I0891329

Trouble Percolates in Coffee City

Center Point
Large Print

Also by James J. Griffin and available from Center Point Large Print:

The Ranger
The Zombies of Zapata
Bullet for a Ranger
Ride for Justice, Ride for Revenge
Trouble Times Two
Desperate Ride
Change of Venue
Death Comes to Lajitas
Catch a Falling Star
Tall Trouble in Terlingua
Rough Riders of the Ragged Rimrock

Trouble Percolates in Coffee City

A Texas Ranger Will Kirkpatrick Novel

JAMES J. GRIFFIN

Center Point Large Print
Thorndike, Maine

This Center Point Large Print edition
is published in the year 2025 by arrangement with
the author.

The text of this Large Print edition is unabridged.
In other aspects, this book may vary
from the original edition.
Printed in the United States of America
on permanent paper sourced using
environmentally responsible foresting methods.
Set in 16-point Times New Roman type.

ISBN: 979-8-89164-576-9

The Library of Congress has cataloged this record
under Library of Congress Control Number: 2025932788

Prologue

Continued from
Rough Riders of the Ragged Rimrock.

Texas Ranger Will Kirkpatrick and his young partner, Jonas Peterson, are stationed at a two-man Ranger outpost in the central Texas town of Sweetwater. From there, they are expected to cover a vast area of central Texas and up into the Panhandle.

On their latest assignment, they had spent many long days and covered many hard miles chasing the notorious Luke Trent gang, a band of seven vicious gunmen who preyed on travelers throughout the wide open, sparsely populated area. They particularly sought out the stagecoaches on which the far-flung small towns and ranches in the region depended for vital transportation and mail services. Trent and his men, ruthless killers all, never left witnesses to their crimes. Even women, children, and the elderly and infirm had fallen victims to their guns.

Will and Jonas finally caught up with the gang just outside the small settlement of Border's Chapel, which later changed its name to Caps.

A fierce gunfight led to the deaths of all seven members of the gang. Will suffered a slight bullet wound to his side, while Jonas was struck on the right side of his head by a bullet, seriously wounding him.

After the gunfight was over, Will called Jonas into the house where he'd confronted the gang leader. Dazed and confused, Jonas came through the door and pointed his gun at Will's stomach, believing him to be the last remaining outlaw.

Will pleaded with his young partner not to gun him down. Jonas shook his head, saying Will had to die for being a woman killer.

He thumbed back the hammer of his Colt and pulled the trigger.

1

Will flinched when Jonas's revolver's hammer dropped, expecting to feel the searing pain of a .45 caliber chunk of hot lead ripping into his gut. Instead, he was still standing. He looked in surprise at Jonas. The gun's hammer had fallen on an empty chamber.

"Son of a bitch!" Jonas muttered. "Don't matter none. I'll kill you with my bare hands."

He tossed the empty gun aside and lunged at Will, grabbing him by the throat. He pressed his thumbs against Will's windpipe, cutting off all his air. Will grew light-headed. Silver spots swam before his eyes as he began to lose consciousness.

Despite his failing strength, Will managed to knee Jonas in the crotch. Jonas groaned, but kept his grip on Will's throat. Will kneed him in the crotch again, harder this time. Jonas yowled in agony. He loosened his grip. Will shoved him backwards as he doubled over. Jonas stared at Will.

"What'd ya do that for, Will?"

Jonas fell to the floor, hands clamped to his crotch. He curled up on his left side and passed out.

Will went to his horse and got his canteen, along with the medical kit and a flask of whiskey from his saddlebags. He uncorked the canteen, took a long swallow of tepid water for himself. He hurried back to Jonas, who was sill unconscious. Will sat alongside him, rolled him onto his back, and held Jonas's head in his lap. He poured some water over Jonas's face. Jonas spluttered. He looked around, confused, as his senses returned.

"Will. Thank God it's you, not Trent or one of his men. What . . . what the hell happened?"

"Here. Take a sip of this first."

Will placed the canteen to Jonas's lips. The young Ranger gulped down water eagerly.

"Not too much now. That's enough."

He pulled the canteen away.

"Do you know who I am?"

"Of course I do, ya damn idjit. Will Kirkpatrick. My Ranger pard, and I thought my friend—even though I'm still in your custody for the next few years. Now tell me what in the blue blazes happened?"

2

Two years previous, Jonas had been forced by his two cousins, Wylie and Kyle, into helping them rob a stagecoach. When Will caught up to them, Wiley made the mistake of going for his gun. Will was forced to shoot him down. The next morning, Kyle managed to trick Will. He knocked Will down and grabbed his gun. The Ranger was helpless, unable to prevent Kyle from shooting him with his own gun.

Jonas, who had resigned himself to his fate, lunged at Kyle, knocking the gun aside at the last moment. In the ensuing struggle for Will's gun between Kyle and Jonas, it went off, killing Kyle. Will was certain Jonas would put a bullet in him and finish him off. Instead, Jonas handed Will his gun back. He willingly let the Ranger take him to jail in Pecos.

At Jonas's trial, he readily admitted his guilt. Will testified in his defense, urging the judge not to sentence him to a long prison term in Huntsville, where the young man would become a hardened criminal, if he even survived confinement in an iron cell behind those high, forbidding walls.

After listening to Will's impassioned plea, the judge agreed Jonas should not go to prison.

However, his terms included a probation of five years, during which time he would be in Will's custody. When Will protested that he couldn't keep watch over Jonas, as his Ranger career kept him on the move, the judge ordered Will to solve the problem by enrolling Jonas in the Rangers. It was either that, or he would be sent to Huntsville. Will gave in. Jonas was sworn in as a Texas Ranger, and assigned as Will's partner.

The decision proved to be a wise one. At the time, Jonas was only seventeen, technically a year too young to be a Ranger recruit. He was green in the techniques of law work, little experienced in the use of guns, knives, or fists. However, he was a quick learner. Within a few months he was adept at all the skills a Ranger would need. He had also, at least twice, saved Will's life. In the time since, he had proved his mettle, and become an invaluable partner to Will, a true man to ride the river with.

3

"Jonas, what's the last thing you remember?"

"Bein' in the middle of one helluva gun battle. Then it got quiet. I heard you callin' me. It sounded like you was in the bottom of a deep well. Then . . . nothing."

"Nothing?"

"Nothing until I woke up lookin' at your ugly face, while you were doin' your damndest to drown me."

"You don't remember coming into this house and tryin' to shoot anyone?"

"No, why? Should I?"

"Lemme take a quick look at your head wound before I answer."

"I got shot in the head?"

"You damn sure did. Not a direct hit, or you wouldn't be talkin' with me right now, instead probably with St. Peter, but a real nasty graze."

"It's funny."

"What's funny?"

"I don't recollect gettin' shot. I still don't hurt anywhere, except my balls. They hurt like hell. Dunno how that happened."

"That's because you took the slug in your thick skull. There's nothing between your ears but solid rock, ya stubborn jackass. Put your hand to the right side of your head."

When Jonas touched the side of his head, he felt the deep groove in the flesh the bullet had left, the missing hair it had burned away. When he pulled his hand back, it was sticky with half dried blood.

"Damn! I guess I did get shot."

"You came damn near gettin' your brains blown out. Let me work on that wound while I fill you in on what happened after the fight was over."

"You mind if I take a swallow of that whiskey before you get to work?"

"As a matter of fact, I do mind, at least until I'm certain you're not gonna pass out on me again. I just brought it along to sterilize the bullet hole before I bandage it."

Will took out his medical kit and opened it. He took off his neckerchief, poured water from his canteen onto it, and began wiping away dried blood, bits of damaged flesh.

"First, in case you haven't realized it, all of Kent's men are dead. Kent, too. He was the last to go down, and he took a whole lot of killin'. Had to put all six bullets in my pistol into him before he went down. Before I could get to him and the other two in the house, they had me pinned down. You shot the door off, and kept me covered while I went through the window. You remember that?"

"Yeah. But nothing afterwards until you dumped that water over my head."

"I called for you. You came into the house,

with kind of a funny look on your face. Sorta like you didn't know where you were at. I'm used to you havin' a blank look in your eyes, but this was different somehow."

"Will, please. This ain't the time for jokes."

"I reckon you're right. I'm sorry. To make a long story short, you thought I was one of Trent's men. Accused me of bein' a son of a bitch woman killer. Said you were gonna make certain I never hurt another woman again. You had your pistol aimed square at the middle of my belly. You planned on gut-shootin' me so I'd die slow. My gun was empty, so there wasn't a damn thing I could do to stop you. I pleaded with you not to shoot me. Kept tryin' to tell you it was me, your pardner, and that I wasn't one of the gang. You wouldn't listen."

"But I didn't pull the trigger, or you wouldn't be here, seems like."

"Oh, you pulled it all right. I figured I was a goner. But your gun was empty, too."

"Then I passed out?"

"Just a minute. This is gonna sting."

Will doused Jonas's wound with whiskey before he answered.

"Nope. You were still bound and determined to kill me. You grabbed me by the throat and tried to choke me to death. Came damn close to succeeding, too. I was just about out of breath when I somehow managed to knee you in the nuts, which is why they hurt, to answer your next question. Had to do that twice before you'd let go. You asked me why I had done that. *Then* you passed out."

"Jeez, Will, I'm sure sorry. I'd never thought I'd try'n kill you."

"Don't worry about it. The bullet must've addled your brain. It seems like you've come out of it. But we need to get you to a doc to make certain."

"So what'll we do now?"

"As far as the Trent gang? Nothing. We'll pull the ones outside into the house, leave those already in the house and bunkhouse where they're at. Once we get back to Sweetwater, I'll send a telegram to the Taylor County sheriff telling him he can go pick up the bodies, if he sees fit to do so. I'm almost done with you. Just got to take a few stitches, put some salve on the wound, and tie a bandage around your head. As long as you feel up to riding, we'll leave soon as we can. We'll take our time, and make the trip in two days, rather than pushing to finish in one. We have to be careful in case you've been hit harder than it seems, and you start getting sick to your stomach, dizzy, or sleepy. That's a sure sign you've got a concussion, mebbe even a brain bleed or a skull fracture. We can't chance makin' it worse if you do."

"Looks like you need a mite of patching up

there yourself, pard," Jonas pointed out, looking at the torn, bloodstained side of Will's shirt.

"Me? That's nothing. Barely a scratch."

Jonas looked at Will with puppy dog eyes and a mournful expression on his face.

"So you're gonna risk getting an infection, becoming real sick or even dying, and leave me to fend for myself with my poor busted head, and my achin' balls that it seems you gave me, thanks ever so much. Some pal you are."

"All right, all right. If it'll make you happy I'll take a look."

Will pulled off his shirt, revealing a long but shallow bullet burn along his left ribcage.

"Looks a mite worse than just a scratch," Jonas said.

"It ain't nothin', but if it'll still make you happy . . ."

"It will."

"Damn mother hen. That's what you are, Jonas."

"Well, I might be, but you damn for certain ain't no cute chick."

Will cleaned out the slash and coated it with salve.

"There. You satisfied now?"

"Yup."

Will got back into his shirt.

"You take it easy while I drag the bodies inside. That's an order," he said, before Jonas could protest. "We'll ride until dusk, then camp for the night. I calculate we'll make about twenty miles tomorrow. That'll leave us only about ten or fifteen the next day, depending on where we stop tomorrow night."

"That sounds fine to me," Jonas agreed.

It didn't take long for Will to drag the dead outlaws into the house, turn their horses loose, then water Pete and Rebel. Once finished, he came for Jonas.

"Let me give you a hand gettin' to your feet, just in case you feel weak or get dizzy."

"I'm obliged."

Will held out his hands, and pulled Jonas upright. Jonas's face flushed, and he swayed for a moment.

"You doin' all right?" Will asked.

"Yeah. I'm fine. Just a little weak, which ain't all that bad, considerin'."

They went out to their horses, Jonas not exactly limping, but kind of shuffling along. When they reached the horses, he hesitated before mounting.

"Something wrong?" Will asked.

"Just preparing myself for the inevitable."

Jonas got his foot in the stirrup, swung his leg over Rebel's rump, and settled into the saddle. He let out a yelp.

"You certain you're all right?"

"Except for the fact my balls hurt like they

were on fire, and feel all swole up, I'm just fine and dandy. I know you did what needed doin' to keep me from killin' you, but I damn sure hope I get the opportunity to return the favor someday."

He patted his bay gelding's shoulder.

"Rebel, if you even think of buckin', or movin' any faster'n a walk, you'll be dog food. That's a promise. You got that, horse?"

Rebel turned his head to look back at his rider, rolled his eyes, and snorted.

"Good boy. Will, I'm as ready to go as I'm gonna be."

"Then let's get started."

Will heeled Pete into a slow walk.

4

Will and Jonas arrived back in Sweetwater late in the morning two days later. Their first stop wasn't at the small building which was their Ranger post. Instead, with Jonas suffering occasional bouts of vertigo and having become so nauseated several times he had to vomit, and Will's wound showing signs of infection, they went directly to Doctor Horace Holcomb's office.

There were no other patients waiting when they arrived. Holcomb was in the small reception area with his wife, looking over a patient's treatment record.

Holcomb was a young man, with only two years of medical practice under his belt. He was about five foot seven, weighing about one hundred and forty-five pounds. He had wavy blond hair and light blue eyes. His manner tended to be cordial, although somewhat brusque.

His wife Marianne contrasted greatly with him, both in appearance and manner. She had deep auburn hair piled high on her head and hazel eyes, was only an inch shorter, and slim, weighing around a hundred and ten. Those eyes always held a cheery sparkle, her lips always upturned in a smile. She could make even the most seriously ill or injured patient feel at least a bit better.

"Mercy sakes. Rangers Kirkpatrick and Peterson. Hello. I'm so happy to see you're back safely," she greeted them.

"Well, not exactly."

Whatever Will was going to say was cut off by Holcomb interrupting him. The physician was more concerned about the bandage wrapped around Jonas's head and Will's bullet-torn, bloodstained shirt than any niceties. Both Rangers also showed flushed faces from the fevers they had developed.

"You men clearly require immediate medical attention. Come into my treatment parlor and let me get to work. Marianne, you'll need to prepare some hot water and sterilize my instruments."

"Of course, Doctor."

"Who needs to be seen first?" Holcomb asked, once they were in the room.

"Jonas," Will answered. "He took a hard bullet graze to the side of his head. I treated it the best I could, but I believe he's got a concussion."

"All right. Ranger Peterson, take off your hat and neckerchief and lie on the table. What are your symptoms?"

"Not too bad, Doc. I get dizzy once in a while, and I've gotten so sick to my stomach I've had to just about puke my guts out a few times."

"I see. Those are rather serious. You may be more badly injured than you realize. Let me take a closer look."

Holcomb lifted Jonas's right eyelid, then his left. "There's one good sign. Your pupils aren't fixed, nor dilated."

He held up his hand.

"How many extended fingers do you see?"

"One."

"Excellent. Now follow that finger with your eyes. Don't move your head."

Holcomb moved his hand up and down, left to right. Jonas's eyes tracked every movement.

"Wonderful," Holcomb said. "Your vision doesn't seem to have been affected. Let me take a closer look at the wound itself."

He washed his hands before unwrapping the bandage, looked critically at the injury.

"You should have had better medical treatment than this much sooner. Who treated this wound?"

"I did," Will answered. "Did the best I could under difficult circumstances. We were more'n two days away from any help."

"Well, I can at last give you credit for trying. Marianne, I'll need that hot water now, along with clean cloths and more carbolic acid."

"Right away, Doctor."

Holcomb picked up a small pair of scissors, dipped them in a pan of carbolic acid, and used them to snip the stitches Will had done to sew Jonas's wound back together. He *tsked* when some pus, along with blood, oozed out of the wound. He next picked up a small pair of needle nosed pliers, sterilized them in the carbolic, and pulled out the stitches.

"Marianne, hot water and cloths, please."

"Certainly, Doctor."

Marianne moved alongside her husband. She held a pan of steaming hot water, with a stack of clean cloths draped over her left arm.

Holcomb took one of the cloths, soaked it, then used it to wipe bits of dried blood, dirt, and dead flesh out of the wound.

He squinted as he looked more closely at it.

"Ranger, I'm going to press on this wound now. It will hurt, but it's absolutely necessary to reach a proper diagnosis. When I do, let me know if you feel any nausea or as if you're going to pass out."

"All right."

After washing his hands again, Holcomb placed both thumbs against the wound and pressed. The bone gave ever so slightly, then came back. Jonas winced, and let out a pained sigh.

"Did you feel any sharp pain, or more like a dull ache, when I pressed, Ranger?" Holcomb asked.

"Just a quick stab, then dull," Jonas answered.

"That's what I thought. You have a slight skull fracture, along with a bit more than just mild concussion. It's not life threatening, unless you develop a blood clot inside your skull, or aggravate the injury. If you develop a clot, I may have to perform a trephination, which is drilling a hole in your skull and removing a small piece of bone to let excess fluid drain out and relieve the pressure."

"That sounds risky, Doc."

"Yeah, Doc. Jonas already has enough holes in his head. He don't need any more," Will said.

"You just stay quiet until it's your turn, Ranger Kirkpatrick," Holcomb scolded, then continued.

"It's more than risky, Ranger Peterson. It's downright dangerous. It's only used as a last resort."

"Then how do you treat me?"

"There isn't really any treatment for this type of injury," Holcomb explained. "All I can do is keep the external wound clean. As far as the fracture and concussion, only time and rest can heal those. You'll need to remain in bed for at least a week, then take things easy after that for another four to six weeks."

"Will I have to stay here?"

"No, you may return home, as long as you get the necessary rest. You really should have someone to care for you, bring your meals, help you stand up and lie back down, things like that. I'll check in every three days to see how you're progressing. Of course, if your condition suddenly worsens, send for me right away."

"Someone to care for me. Hmmm. I wonder who that might be?"

Jonas looked directly at Will.

"I . . . I suppose I could," Will stammered.

"I'd be obliged, pardner."

"Excellent," Holcomb said. "I'll finish working on you, then check Ranger Kirkpatrick."

Once Holcomb had Jonas all bandaged up, he turned his attention to Will. He had him sit on the table and remove his shirt.

Once again, Holcomb *tsked* when he saw Will's wound.

"This really needs stitches."

"I don't think so," Will objected. "I patched myself up pretty good."

"Who's the doctor here, Ranger, and who's the patient?"

"Um. You are, Doc. I guess that makes me the patient."

"Then you stick to law work, and let me tend to medical issues."

"I told him he needed some da . . . uh, dang stitches," Jonas said, catching himself and not swearing in front of Mrs. Holcomb. "He wouldn't hear of it."

"Well, he's getting some now, whether he likes it or not," Holcomb said.

Will merely sighed in resignation.

Holcomb went to work, cleaning the wound, sewing it up with fifteen stitches, then dressing it.

"Don't do anything too strenuous, so you don't break those stitches open," he warned.

"That means I can't help Jonas get up and down, right, Doc?" Will asked, as he shrugged back into his shirt.

Jonas's face fell.

"Not at all. As long as you don't exert yourself too much, or twist the wrong way, you should have no issues."

This time, Will's face fell, while Jonas's brightened considerably.

"You're both set to leave now. I'll be by at eight o'clock Thursday morning to check on the two of you, change the bandages and dressings. Until then, rest as much as possible. Eat as normal a diet as you feel like. If either of you feel sick, or start developing a higher fever than you have right now, come back to see me immediately."

"We'll do that," Jonas promised.

"How much do we owe you?" Will asked.

"Three dollars for Ranger Peterson, two for Ranger Kirkpatrick. It will also be two dollars apiece for the house call on Thursday. You can pay me then. I'll bring a receipt for both days, that you will be able to turn in for reimbursement. If there's nothing else, I do have other patients scheduled for after I have my noontime dinner and rest."

"Nothing else for us, Doc," Will said. "We're obliged."

"Yeah, Doc. I'm mighty grateful," Jonas added. "See you in three days."

After leaving Doctor Holcomb's office, Will and Jonas stopped at the Sweetwater Café for a meal of beefsteaks, fried potatoes, black-eyed peas, and dried apple pie, washed down with several cups of strong black coffee. Once they finished their meal, they cared for their horses. After that they went inside.

"There's nothin' that can't wait until tomorrow," Will said.

He unbuckled his gun belt and set it on the table between the beds, sat on the edge of his mattress, pulled off his boots, and stretched out on his back.

"Hey, pard, ain't ya gonna help me get in bed?" Jonas asked.

"You really need help?"

"You heard what the doc said. And it's the least you can do after squashin' my nuts flatter'n a pancake."

"Which I had to do to keep you from killin' me. You're lucky flattenin' 'em's all I did. I should've torn 'em clean off."

"All right, I'll concede the point," Jonas said. "Besides, if anyone's gonna help me into bed, it'll be Susannah from Polly's Parlor of Pleasure."

"Uh-uh. Doc Holcomb said take it easy, remember?"

"Yeah. I guess Susannah will wait."

Jonas also removed his gun belt and boots, then got into bed. Within minutes, both men were sound asleep.

5

Will and Jonas spent the next three days resting, doing little but caring for the horses, eating and sleeping. As he'd promised, Doctor Holcomb came by on Thursday to check on them and tend to their wounds. He pronounced both men healing more rapidly than he'd dared hope.

Will took advantage of the respite to take care of some long overdue paperwork. He completed reports on every case he and Jonas had covered over the past two months, up to and including the deaths of Luke Trent and his comrades in crime. When he'd signed the last one, he leaned back in his chair, yawned and stretched.

"Finally done," he said.

"You could've let me help you some," Jonas said.

"Uh-uh." Will shook his head. "Straining your eyes doin' all this reading and writing would've only given you a worse headache than the ones you've been havin'."

"The doc told me to expect those for a while," Jonas said.

"I know, but why take a chance on making them worse? It's not like I had much else to do. Monday mornin' I'll take a walk over to the Post Office and send these off to Austin."

"You've got quite a pile there. Don't forget to tuck the doctor's receipts in with those reports so we get our money back."

"Already got them on the stack."

With the weekend upon them, Sweetwater became livelier, with ranch hands coming in from the surrounding spreads. Will did visit the city marshal to offer his assistance if needed, but was assured by Luke Zimmerman he and his deputies could handle any trouble. With Sweetwater being the seat of Nolan County, the county sheriff could also be called on for assistance if needed. Will picked up two bottles of Old Grand-Dad at the High Plains Saloon. He brought those back to the post, where he and Jonas would drink them while playing a few hands of poker, away from any possible trouble.

Friday and Saturday came and went uneventfully. Sunday morning, Will and Jonas decided to go to services at the Sweetwater Community Union Church. They rarely got to church, both being religious men and strong believers in God Almighty, but not particularly fond of any particular denomination. They felt the Almighty's presence more strongly out in the wide open, riding their horses, than in any man-made building. When in a town, they would simply choose the nearest church, on occasion even a Catholic mission. Despite feeling out of place, especially since they always had to wear their guns, often without revealing their true identities as Texas Rangers, they were almost universally made welcome, and generally enjoyed the services. Neither had been granted good singing voices by the Lord, so they were content to just listen to the choir singing. Of course, the after-service refreshments and fellowship were also a treat.

After Doctor Holcomb tended to them again on Monday morning, allowing Jonas a bit more activity, they walked to the Post Office. After mailing the reports, finding no mail from Headquarters waiting, they went over to the café for a leisurely breakfast. Afterwards, they went back to the post, pulled their chairs outside, and sat in front of the post, soaking up the sunshine and watching the passersby.

The next morning, Sheriff Max Quiello knocked on their door just after sunrise.

"Who is it?" Will called, still in bed and half asleep. Jonas hadn't stirred.

"It's the sheriff. Come to ask you a favor, Ranger."

"I'll be right there."

Will dragged himself out of his bunk and, shirtless and barefoot, padded to the door and opened it.

"Sorry to wake you so early," Quiello apologized. "May I come in?"

"Come on in."

Will swung the door wide.

Jonas finally awakened.

"Who's here, Will?"

"The sheriff."

"Don't bother to get up, Jonas. I know you were bad hurt rounding up the Trent bunch," Quiello said.

"It's high time I was out of bed anyway," Jonas grumbled. "Me'n Will are gettin' fat and lazy, just hanging around all day and doin' nothing. Hell, even our horses are packing on the pounds. We need to get back to work."

"I'm sorry the coffee's not on yet, Max," Will apologized. "We weren't expecting company. What brings you by?"

"I hate to ask you this, but are you feeling up to givin' me a hand?"

Will shrugged.

"That depends. I might be able to, but Jonas ain't gonna be fit to get back in the saddle for a week or two more. Why do you ask?"

"Last night, Tom Hutchings got all liquored up at the High Plains. He got into an argument with another cowboy, Lank Purdy. Beat him up real bad. Doc Holcomb says Purdy might well be crippled for the rest of his life."

"Tom Hutchings? Troy Hutchings' oldest boy?"

"That's the one. He always has been trouble. He cut a lick for home soon as Purdy hit the floor.

My deputy Frank Eddy went after him. Frank's horse came back this morning. Frank didn't. There was blood all over the saddle."

"So it appears one of the Hutchings killed your deputy," Will said.

"That or shot him bad enough he couldn't stay in the saddle," Quiello answered. "I'm ridin' out to the Slash H now, to bring Tom in. I'm takin' Frank's horse along to bring him back home. With any luck he'll just be shot bad, but still alive. I might have to arrest Tom's pa or one of his brothers, too, depending. All my other deputies are spread all over the county. I'm lookin' for a man to side me."

"Say no more," Jonas said.

"You just rein in there," Will said. "You know you ain't in any shape to go after a wanted man, perhaps get into another shooting scrape. If you get a dizzy spell you might get yourself, or me or the sheriff, killed. You'll stay right here. That's an order."

"What if you and the sheriff don't come back, Will?"

"Then I guess you'll be givin' the orders to yourself, so you can do whatever you damn well please."

"I reckon I don't have much choice. You be careful, Will. You ain't healed up all the way yet neither. The same goes for you, Max. Good luck."

"I will be," Quiello assured him.

"Let's quit wasting time," Will said. He grabbed his socks and boots, pulled them on, then took his shirt from its peg and slid it on, tucking it into his denims. He picked up his gun belt and buckled it around his waist, lifting his Colt from its holster, checking the gun's action, and putting a shell into the empty chamber under the hammer. He tied his bandanna loosely around his neck, and jammed his hat on his head.

"Let's ride, Max."

6

It was just over six miles to the Slash H Ranch. Four miles along, Will spotted buzzards circling in slow descent, their black bodies stark against the clear blue sky.

"Max."

Will pointed at the winged scavengers.

"I see the damn things," Quiello replied, his voice tight. "I reckon we've found Frank."

He put his horse into a gallop, with Will at his side. When they reached the spot where the buzzards had now landed, Quiello pulled out his rifle and shot one of the winged scavengers. Black feathers flew everywhere.

"Damn you. Let Frank in peace, you feathered bastards."

He shot another as it rose into the sky. It plunged to the ground, trailing feathers. The rest scattered, squawking in protest.

"Easy, Max," Will said. "You don't want to give us away by letting the Hutchings hear those shots."

Quiello shoved his Winchester back into its scabbard. His voice was quavering with emotion, his eyes moist.

"You're right. Let's take care of poor Frank, then get after that son of a bitch who killed him."

The deputy was lying just off the side of the road, face up in a clump of prickly pear, his blood staining the plant's pads and bright yellow flowers. The buzzards had already done a good deal of their grisly work. Eddy's eyes were gone, just the sockets remaining where they had been. His belly was ripped open, most of the internal organs gone. There was a bullet hole in the center of his chest.

Will and Quiello dismounted.

"Give me a few moments alone with Frank, will you, Ranger?"

"Of course. I want to look around for any evidence. I'll do that. It'll probably take me around twenty minutes."

"That'll be fine."

Quiello knelt alongside Eddy's body. He removed his hat, buried his face in his hands. His body shook as deep sobs wracked it.

Will walked around, examining the area. Atop a low rise, he found an ejected rifle cartridge, observed where a man had knelt on one knee in waiting, and removed a length of red-checked cloth caught on a mesquite's thorny branch.

By the time he returned to Quiello, the sheriff had wrapped Eddy's body in a blanket, draped it belly down over the deputy's horse, and tied it in place. He had a lead rope tied from Eddy's grulla gelding to his saddle horn.

"You find anything, Will?"

"I sure did. Tom Hutchings knew someone would come after him. He didn't go straight home. He hid himself on top of that rise yonder and waited. He shot your deputy from ambush. It was cold-blooded, cowardly murder. I recovered an empty cartridge casing, saw where Hutchings had knelt, and this."

He showed Quiello the scrap of cloth.

Quiello snorted.

"That doesn't prove anything. It doesn't even tie Tom to the killing."

"It does if I can find the shirt this came from. We just have to hope he hasn't gotten rid of the shirt. And that his pa doesn't insist on a search warrant. By the time we got one, you can be damn certain that shirt will have been burned."

"Even so, it's still mighty flimsy evidence. Purely circumstantial."

"It's more than we started with," Will pointed out.

"You're right. Let's go get that bastard."

No one was in sight when they rode up to the main house at the Slash H. They stopped in front of the rambling cedar and adobe structure, dismounted, and tied their horses to three of the several iron horsehead hitching posts. They stepped onto the verandah, and huddled against the thick adobe wall.

“It’s awful quiet,” Will said.

“Too quiet,” Quiello agreed. “You reckon they’re waiting to blast us to Kingdom Come as soon as we walk through that door?”

“I’d bet my hat they are,” Will answered. “And I’m mighty fond of my hat. I’m kind of surprised they haven’t started shooting already, or at least come out to warn us to get off their place. Remind me again how many of ’em we’ll be up against.”

“It depends on how old Troy reacts. Word’s goin’ around he’s getting tired of Tom’s troublemaking. Worried Tom might bring trouble down on the whole family. If we have to face the entire brood, there’s Troy, who’s a tough old bird, Tom, the one we’ve come for, and four other boys. One of those, Gary, is going to school somewhere back East, so he shouldn’t be around.”

“So five against two. Plus however many of the ranch hands decide to take a hand in this game. For all we know, there could be a dozen rifles pointed at us right now.”

“That’s the other thing,” Quiello said. “There doesn’t seem to be any activity in the bunkhouse, stables, or corrals. Not even the smithy. There should be at least a few workers here. Of course, most of the men could be out mendin’ fences, looking for lost calves or stray cattle. Could even be doctorin’ cows or castrating calves.”

“Let’s not worry about those *hombres* until

we have to," Will said. "Any women about the place?"

"Just one, an old Scottish woman who's the cook, maid, and housekeeper. Tom's wife, Mildred, died giving birth to Bobby, the youngest. They never had a daughter. Mildred was the one who kept Tom in check, at least the best she could. When she passed, Tom went on a tear for two weeks. He blamed the poor baby for him losing his mother. Even said he'd like to see Bobby dead, more than once. I think the only reason Tom hasn't killed his baby brother was he's well aware then his father would kill him."

"We've been out here talking for nigh unto five minutes and still no sign of anyone stirring," Will said. "There's no point in wasting any more time. Let's go in there. You stay on the right side of the door, I'll take the left. I'll knock and see if one of the Hutchings answers, or they answer with lead."

"I thought you were helpin' me," Quiello said, chuckling. "Seems like things have turned around, and you've taken over."

"I'm sorry. Force of habit," Will apologized.

"Don't be, I'm kind of glad you are. Lets me off the hook if anything goes wrong. Also means I might even get re-elected to another term come next election. Let's make our move."

Both men took out their revolvers. Will rapped

on the thick cedar door with the barrel of his. There was no answer. He rapped on the door again, harder. Still no answer.

He looked at Quiello and shook his head, then stepped in front of the door. He tried to open it, but it was locked. He kicked at it, once, twice, a third time. There was still not a sound from inside. He looked at Quiello, shook his head, and kicked again. It took three more times before the latch finally gave way and the door swung inward. Guns at the ready, they stepped through the door. No one was in sight. The house was strangely silent.

"We'd better start searching the rooms," Will whispered. "Have you even been in this house before?"

Quiello shook his head. "Only as far as this here foyer."

"Then we'd better stick together, until we get the layout."

Will and the sheriff worked their way through the house. There was no one in the parlor, sitting room, or library. No one was in the dining room, no sign of anyone having been there for breakfast. Even the table was bare, with no covering or place settings. The kitchen was empty, the stove cold, no food on the counters ready to be prepared.

"The bedrooms," Quiello said.

Will nodded silent agreement.

A long corridor off the dining room led to the sleeping quarters.

"You take the right, I'll take the left," Will said.

"All right."

Guns still at the ready, they started down the hall. Will opened the door to the first room on his side. As he did, a shotgun blast roared. Sheriff Quiello fell backwards from the doorway of the opposite room, the entire right side of his body riddled with buckshot from his hip to his shoulder. He landed on his back, his only movement the twitching of one leg, reaction from nerves which didn't realize they were already dead.

Will spun and dove to his belly just in time to avoid having his guts blown out or head torn off by a second shotgun blast, the buckshot blowing a hole in the wall behind where he'd just been standing. He landed atop the dead sheriff, rolled off, and emptied his pistol into the room from which the shotgun blasts had come. He heard the dull thud of lead hitting flesh, the grunts as each bullet found its target. He heard the clatter of the shotgun bouncing off something metallic, the squeaking of bedsprings, the thump of a body hitting the floor.

Will got to his feet, and once he stood up, slipped on the blood-slicked floor. He caught himself, using one hand against the wall to steady himself. He didn't bother to check on the sheriff. No man could survive taking a direct hit of ten-gauge buckshot at point blank range. He stepped into the bedroom. Tom Hutchings was lying face down on the floor, the back of his shirt torn and bloodied from three exit wounds. The covers on the brass bed were also bloodied, the wall behind it pockmarked with bullet holes from Will's slugs, which had torn through Hutchings, then buried themselves in the wall. Hutchings' still smoking shotgun was on the floor at the foot of the bed.

Will reloaded his gun, then, using the toe of his boot, rolled Hutchings onto his back. Four of his six bullets had found their mark, two just to the right of Hutchings' belly button, two in the center of his chest. His eyes were wide open, not in shock or pain, but what looked to Will to be an expression of amazement. Will left the body where it lay and left the room, closing the door behind him.

A chunk of ice seemed to settle in Will's stomach, his throat tightening as if clamped in a vise. He uttered a silent prayer, hoping against all hope he wouldn't find what he dreaded.

He went into the next bedroom. Two of the other Hutchings boys were lying in their beds, their faces nothing but masks of unrecognizable pulp from being hit with shotgun blasts at close range. Will backed out of the room, closing the door behind him.

The next room yielded almost the same result. The last boy was lying in his bed, his face blown away.

The next room was empty, either belonging to Gary, the boy away at college, or Tom.

There were two rooms left. Will sucked in a deep breath, and opened the door to the nearest one.

Troy Hutchings was in it. He hadn't been shot in the face, nor been in bed. He was sprawled next to a tipped over chair where he'd been shot twice in the chest with the same shotgun that killed the others. Also in the room was the body of the Scottish housekeeper and cook. She'd been shot in the back with a pistol. Near her was a silver tray, shattered crockery, and spilled food. It appeared she had been bringing Troy his breakfast when they'd been ambushed.

Will was used to seeing violent death, but nothing else he'd ever seen, not even the victims of Indian attacks, rivaled this. He had to get outside, fast. He slammed Troy's door shut and left the house as quickly as possible. He stopped on the verandah. With shaking hands, he managed to roll and light a quirly. He sucked smoke deep into his lungs to steady his nerves.

There was still one more question to be answered. Where were all the ranch hands? Will had an idea, but it needed to be confirmed.

He took one more drag on his quirly, tossed

the butt into the dirt and ground it out under his bootheel. He crossed the yard to the bunkhouse, hesitated for a moment, then opened the door.

The scene which greeted him was far worse than he'd even imagined. At the far end of the bunkhouse's main room, the bodies of at least twenty men were haphazardly stacked up against the wall like cordwood. Thousands of flies were already feeding on the bloodied corpses, their buzzing so loud the building itself seemed to vibrate. It appeared Tom had caught the men by surprise, probably when they were still asleep, then herded them to the back of the building, where he shotgunned the entire crew in an act of wanton slaughter.

Will staggered outside, dropped to his knees, and violently vomited, emptying the contents of his stomach. He crawled a few feet, rolled onto his back, and gulped in huge draughts of fresh air. Even for the veteran Ranger, the gruesome scene was rough to comprehend.

Will lay there until he felt he'd regained enough strength to resume working. On wobbly legs, he returned to the house. He grabbed Sheriff Quiello by the wrists and dragged the lifeless local lawman outside. He took a blanket from Quiello's bedroll, wrapped the sheriff in it, then attempted to toss Quiello onto his blue roan gelding. The horse shied, terrified by the sights and odors of blood and death. It took Will fifteen minutes of speaking softly and gently stroking the horse's neck before he could convince it to stand still enough to allow him to drape Quiello belly down over his saddle and lash him in place.

Will took the time to lean against Pete, light another quirly, and smoke it before mounting his paint and starting back to town. Several times on the way, he closed his eyes, trying to force the images of the massacre at the Slash H out of his mind.

7

It was after dark when Will returned to the Ranger post. Jonas was asleep in his bunk. He stirred when he heard Will open the door.

"Will? That you? What the hell time is it?"

"About nine o'clock."

"Where in the blue blazes have you been? I've got news."

"It's a long story."

Jonas rolled over, broke a lucifer from the bundle he'd left on the bedside table, struck it to life. He lifted the chimney from the coal oil lamp, touched the match to the wick and lit it. He slid the chimney back in place, and as the lamp's flame grew brighter he looked at Will.

"What happened to you, pardner? You look like a horse that's been rode hard and put up wet. As if you've been through Hell and back."

"I pretty much have been."

Will walked over to the corner cabinet, took out a three quarters full bottle of Old Grand-Dad. He uncorked the bottle and took three long swallows.

"You said you had news?"

"It can wait. Tell me what happened."

Will sat on the edge of his bunk and took another slug of whiskey. He rolled and lit a quirly before answering.

"I'll keep it short. We found the deputy's body about two miles before the Hutchings' spread. He'd been ambushed. After we picked him up we went on to the ranch. No one seemed to be there."

Will stopped and took another swig from the bottle and drag on his smoke.

"There didn't seem to be anyone around anywhere. The house, the bunkhouse, the barns, nowhere. Me'n the sheriff went inside the main house and started searching. We didn't find anyone until we came to the bedrooms. Tom Hutchings was hiding in one of 'em. As soon as Max opened the door, Hutchings blew him away with a shotgun. Tore Max to pieces. I dove to the floor just in time to avoid taking the second barrel right in my face. Then I emptied my six-gun into Tom. Got him four times. The other two slugs missed, but it turned out that didn't matter. I killed him deader'n a three-day old fish out of water."

"You didn't get hit? You look awful bloody."

Will shook his head.

"No, when I ducked that shotgun I landed on Max. I'm covered in his blood."

"Boy howdy, no wonder you look awful. It's a shame about Max, too. He was a good man."

"It gets worse. When I searched the rest of the house, everyone else was dead. Tom's brothers, his father, even the housekeeper. He'd killed every last one of them with that damn shotgun. Except the housekeeper. He shot her in the back with his pistol."

"His entire family?"

"Yep. His entire family."

"Damn."

Will took yet another drink.

"I'm not finished. When I checked the bunkhouse, all the ranch hands were dead. He'd herded every last man to one end of the room, then riddled them with buckshot. He didn't leave one man alive. There was blood everywhere, and the damn flies . . ."

Will's voice trailed off.

"Twenty-one men, plus his family."

"I'm sorry I wasn't with you, Will."

"There was nothing you could've done anyway. It was the worst massacre I've ever seen. Worse even than any Indian raids I've dealt with. I'm not ashamed to say I puked my damn guts out."

"Are the bodies still out there?"

"Yeah, except for Max and Frank Eddy, the deputy. I brought them back and left them with the undertaker. One of Quiello's other deputies returned while I was doin' that. He's gonna take some men out to the Slash H come morning and bring the rest of the bodies back to town. He's also goin' to get word to Gary Hutchings, the only one left. He's at college back East, or Tom would've killed him, too."

"You gonna be all right? Want me to brew some coffee or fix some ham and eggs?"

"No. My stomach couldn't handle food right now. What's this news you said you've got?"

"We've received new orders."

Will looked at Jonas. He shook his head.

"We've got new orders?"

"Sure do. We're headed for the Border."

"The Border? We're abandoning our post here?"

"Not abandoning it. Just closing it temporarily."

"Why the devil are we being sent to the damn Border?"

"To capture *El Atrevido*."

"*El Atrevido*? The Daring One? Who the hell is *El Atrevido*?"

Jonas held out a yellow Western Union flimsy.

"Read this."

"You'd better read it to me. My eyes are kind of blurry."

"Sure. *El Atrevido* is a Mexican *bandido*. He and his gang have been raising Cain along the Border for some time now. It seems they've taken over a small Border town name of Coffee City. Since there's no other Rangers available right now, the job falls to us, pard."

"It's nigh unto a three-hundred-mile ride just to get there," Will said. "And that's riding damn hard, through some of the most rugged and isolated land in the entire state."

"That's only the half of it. No one seems to know what this *El Atrevido* looks like. Every description of him is different."

"Wonderful."

"It gets worse. A lot of the Mexicans in the region look on this *El Atrevido* as some kind of folk hero. Kind of a Mexican Robin Hood. You know, rob from the rich *Yanqui gringos* and give to the poor peons."

"So we'll not only be up against this *hombre*, but most of the population."

"That's right. We can't count on any help, not even from the local law."

Will shook his head.

"That's plenty for now. I've had enough of this day. You can give me the rest of the details tomorrow."

Will emptied the bottle of Old Grand-Dad, then fell on his back, crossways over his mattress. The loud snores of a man who'd passed out from too much hard liquor soon reverberated through the room.

8

After tying up loose ends, Will and Jonas went to the Sweetwater Mercantile, where they picked up needed supplies for their long journey south. They had already locked up the Ranger post, and in case of emergency, left a spare key with Hal Boyle, the deputy sheriff on duty. It was close to ten o'clock before they rode out.

Truth to tell, it was Jonas who had actually done most of the tying up, along with purchasing the supplies. He even had to saddle and bridle Will's horse for him. Pete had looked at his rider in disgust when it took Will three tries to get his foot in the stirrup and pull himself onto the paint's back. The last attempt had almost ended in disaster. Will got halfway into the saddle, then flopped belly down into the seat. He hung on, dizzy, until his head stopped spinning and his stomach stopped churning. After five minutes, he managed to swing his leg over Pete's rump and settle into the saddle. Jonas just looked at him and shook his head. This would not be the time to burst out laughing, although he was sorely tempted.

Will was suffering from the worst hangover of his life. In addition, he couldn't shake the horrific images of the massacre at the Slash H. The only reason he'd slept through the night, until Jonas shook him awake, was the quantity of liquor he'd imbibed. His head was pounding, his mouth dry as an old cotton sock. His stomach threatened to leap up into his throat at any moment. Each step Pete took, even at the slow pace they were setting, brought renewed waves of agony. Jonas wisely stayed silent, knowing the only cure for what ailed his partner was time.

Their route would take them almost due south for nearly two hundred and fifty miles to Del Rio. From there, it was another forty miles northwest to Coffee City. The only major settlement they would pass through en route was San Angelo, about seventy-five miles south of Sweetwater. They would reach there in two days, possibly their only chance to spend the night in a hotel room until they reached Del Rio.

This section of the trip went through high, arid plains, the only features an occasional low rise or eroded mesa. While not as flat or featureless as the *Llano Estacado* to the north and west, the barren land, covered only with low, drought-hardy shrubs, grasses, and cactus, showed no mercy to the travelers. There was no shade to provide relief from the blazing Texas sun, few sources of water, only miles of monotony. Even most of the animals were seldom seen, roadrunners and snakes, a few species of songbirds, javelinas, and feral boars. Most of the longhorns had long since been rounded up, but those boars, if aroused, could present even more of a danger to the unwary. Short-tempered, with dim eyesight, keen senses of smell and hearing, almost anything could incur their anger. The boars' long tusks could eviscerate a horse or a man. They would then tear the hapless victim to pieces in a feeding frenzy.

About two o'clock, the Rangers stopped at a small waterhole to give themselves and their horses a break. As always, the animals were cared for first, allowed to drink, then crop at the sparse grass. After they filled their canteens, Will removed his hat and bandanna, stretched out on his belly, and dipped his face into the refreshing water. Once done, he dunked the bandanna into the pool, let it soak, then ran it over his chest and shoulders, letting the water drench his shirt. The garment would soon dry out, but while it was damp it would provide at least a short while of relief.

"You feelin' any better?" Jonas asked.

"Considerably. I'm sorry I've been lousy company today," Will answered.

"No need to apologize. You had a damn fine reason to get good and drunk. Hell, I doubt if I'd have been able to handle the situation any better than you did. Probably not."

"A lawman ain't supposed to let his damn emotions get in the way of his work."

"Like you told me once, Will, a lawman's only human. It's a tough job we have, and sometimes it just gets to us. You've got no reason to be ashamed. Hell, you saw a man get shot almost in two right in front of you. And you nearly got it the same way. You're lucky to be here with me at all. On top of all that, you had to deal with what Tom Hutchings did, butcher his family and a whole passel of others. It'll take time, but you'll be fine."

"I figure I'd better be before we get to Coffee City, and have to run down *El Atrevido* and his bunch."

"And with a whole lot of folks he's duped into thinking he's out for them, not himself and his band of cutthroats. A lot of those will be just achin' to put a knife or a bullet in our backs."

"You've got a unique way of trying to make a feller feel better, Jonas."

"*Gracias*. It's just one of my many talents. Now, are we gonna talk away the entire afternoon, or are you ready to get some food in your belly?"

"My belly says it's not ready to stomach food," Will said with a slight smile. "But I've gotta get something in it, like it or not. Now's as good a time as any."

"Another so-called joke like that and you'll have somethin' in your belly all right," Jonas said. "My fist, about four inches deep into your guts."

"Not today. I couldn't handle that," Will said. "So what've we got? The usual jerky and hard-tack?"

Jonas put on a false British accent.

"Why no, my dear fellow. How uncouth of you. I feel insulted. I purchased for us a marvelous repast of the finest victuals at the most exclusive dining establishment in the metropolis of Sweetwater, Texas. In my saddlebags I have hard-boiled eggs, the finest imported Polish ham and Swiss cheese on crusty loaves of freshly baked bread, pickles, and even sugar cookies to conclude our meal. All to be washed down with a fine vintage of sarsaparilla. Tut, tut. I know you are going to protest, fine sir, but they were all out of French champagne. I don't believe your delicate constitution could handle the bubbly at this moment in any event. I'm positive the sarsaparilla will prove most satisfactory. If you prefer when I open the bottles you may sniff the bouquet."

"Just produce the grub before you find *my* fist in *your* guts," Will said, laughing.

"That sounds more like the Will Kirkpatrick I know, the wealthy banker's son," Jonas said.

"Never mind that."

"All right, Master Kirkpatrick. Let us dine, henceforth."

• • •

"That was indeed some good chuck," Will said, once they'd finished eating. "What do you have planned for tonight?"

"A mixed grill of bacon, beans, and biscuits. For tomorrow morning, bacon and biscuits. At noon or thereabouts, beef jerky and hardtack. Tomorrow evening, for a change of pace we shall have beans, biscuits, and bacon."

"We'll be in San Angelo tomorrow night," Will reminded him. "I dunno about you, but I'm planning on a nice thick, juicy steak with all the fixin's at a decent restaurant."

"And thank God for that," Jonas answered. "Bacon and beans does get mighty tiresome right quick. Let's get on our ponies and ride. *El Atrevido* awaits the pleasure of our company. We must not keep him waiting. Let us sally forth, post haste."

Will shot him a dirty look.

"*Tally ho,* then."

9

The segment of Will and Jonas's trip from Sweetwater to San Angelo was uneventful. While this was Jonas's first time in the city, Will had been there several times previously.

"There's a good livery stable a few blocks ahead, Jonas. I also like to stay at the Concho Hotel. It's not fancy, but it's clean and quiet."

"Pretty much any hotel's better than sleeping on the hard ground, Will. Although I've been in a few where I should've just camped outside of town, or slept in the livery stable's damn hayloft. I'm more interested in where we're gonna eat tonight."

"I've been in some of those same kind of hotels," Will said, laughing. "There's an excellent restaurant two blocks from the hotel. It's called the Mid-Texas Steakhouse. I've always gotten a good meal there. Thick, juicy steaks, fried taters, fresh vegetables if they're in season, and the best coffee I've ever tasted."

"Stop. My belly's complaining enough already. Don't talk about food until we get to the restaurant."

"You don't want to hear about the pies and cakes?"

"Nope. Just want to eat some . . . of each."

Jonas put Rebel into a trot. Will urged Pete to keep up.

The owner of the San Angelo Horse Haven Livery Stable was sitting on an empty nail keg in front of the barn, idly passing the time by whittling. When he heard the approaching riders, he looked up and recognized Will.

"Doggone! As I live and breathe, if it ain't Ranger Will Kirkpatrick. Dadgum it, it's been a long time. Where in the blue blazes have you been keepin' yourself? Who's your friend?"

"One question at a time, Charlie," Will answered. "I haven't been keeping myself anywhere. I go where the Rangers send me. Right now I'm stationed at a post up to Sweetwater."

"Sweetwater! San Angelo's a helluva long way from Sweetwater."

"It's only a two-day ride, but I know you're not fond of traveling. Have you ever even been outside of San Angelo?"

"Just once. Got as far as Vancourt. Got homesick so I turned right around and came back home. Never left San Angelo since. You still haven't told me who your friend is."

"This mean lookin' young *hombre*? He's my pardner, Jonas Peterson. The reason we're headed south is we've taken on a temporary assignment. I can't say more than that."

"Hell, Will. You can tell me. You know I can keep my mouth shut."

Will threw back his head and laughed.

"You? Keep a secret, Charlie? Hell, if I told you anything, it'd be all over this damn town before we even had the saddles off of our horses. I hope you've got a couple of empty stalls for them."

"I sure do. Get down. Light and set a spell. Give those broncs' backs a rest."

Will and Jonas dismounted.

Charlie Hayes was somewhere north of fifty. He was short, only about five foot five, and weighed less than one hundred forty pounds. He had long gray hair, brown eyes, and a tobacco stained long gray beard. His grip was firm as he took Jonas's hand.

"I'm mighty pleased to meet you, young feller. Will, he's not mean lookin' a'tall. Seems like a real nice *hombre*. Call me Charlie, son. You don't mind if I call you Jonas? I like the looks of your horse, too. What d'ya call him?"

"I'm pleased to meet you, too, Charlie."

Jonas had to shake his hand to get feeling back into it once Charlie released his grip.

"This here's Rebel. He's a mighty good horse. Tough, level-headed. Has plenty of bottom, and can run like the devil himself was after him when he needs to. Scared of nothing except missing a meal."

"Kind of like his owner," Will broke in.

"Sounds an awful lot like another certain Ranger I could name, and that same Ranger's horse, Will Kirkpatrick."

"All right. Ya got me, Charlie."

"Pete's still lookin' mighty fine, Will."

"We take care of each other. He's still a beggar, though."

"Pie biters and biscuit eaters are made by their owners. You spoil that horse, Will. I'd wager Jonas spoils his, too."

"Now ya got me, Charlie," Jonas said with a chuckle.

"Let's get down to business. How long are you gonna need those stalls?"

"Just for tonight," Will answered. "We'll be riding out first thing tomorrow morning. The usual. Grain, water, all the hay they can eat, a good rubdown and grooming."

"Do you need me to bring 'em to the farrier to have their shoes checked?"

"Not unless you find any loose ones when you groom them. We had them reshod before we left Sweetwater. We'll have that done again when we reach Del . . . um, where we're headed."

Will caught himself, too late. A sly gleam came into Charlie's eyes.

"Of course. Where you're headed. As far as my rates, they haven't changed. Six bits a night."

"That's fine."

Will dug in his pocket, removed two silver

dollars, and handed them to the livery owner. Charlie bit them to make certain they were genuine.

"Keep the change," Will told him. "Jonas, you can pay me back by buying the first couple of drinks tonight."

"Okay by me."

"Get the gear you need off your broncs so I can get to work on 'em," Charlie ordered. "You staying at the Concho, as usual?"

"Sure am. It's the only decent hotel in this town. Jonas, grab your stuff so we can get our room, clean up, then chow down on some good grub."

"Got it."

Will and Jonas untied their saddlebags and slung them over their shoulders. They took their Winchesters from the saddle scabbards and toted them along.

"See you in the morning, Charlie," Will said. "About seven."

"Your horses will be ready," Charlie assured him. "*Manana*."

The only rooms available at the Concho Hotel were on the first floor, in the front of the building. This meant the Rangers would be subjected to the noise and dust from the street and boardwalk until the early hours of the morning. Jonas suggested they try another hotel, but Will said no. He explained that the Concho was still the best choice. The alternatives would be one of the other hotels, none of which were as clean or quiet as the Concho, or the hayloft at Charlie's livery stable. Compared to what was ahead of them, a noisy, dusty room would be downright paradise by comparison.

After paying the desk clerk, they went down the corridor to Room 110.

"This isn't all that bad," Jonas said. "It's awful damn stuffy in here, though. You think I should open the window?"

Will shook his head.

"I wouldn't. That'll only let more dust and noise into the room, but won't cool it off much. We can always open it later if gets unbearable. Mebbe once the sun goes down."

"Are we headed straight for supper?" Jonas asked. "I'm plumb starved."

"Soon as we wash up some," Will answered. "Boy howdy, I'd purely enjoy a nice hot bath, shave, and a haircut, but we don't have time for those. With eight more days of riding ahead of us, that'd just be a waste of time and money in any event. Two hours after we started out, we'd be just as dirty and sweaty as we are right now anyway. Do you want to wash up first, or should I go ahead?"

"You go ahead. I'll test out the mattress while you do that."

Jonas pulled off his boots and hat, then flopped on the bed.

"Nice and comfy. The pillows are real soft."

"Just don't forget one of 'em's mine."

Will took off his vest, hat, and bandanna. He unbuttoned his shirt, walked over to the washstand. He poured water from the pitcher into the basin, and ducked his face and hair into the refreshing liquid.

He took the bar of Pears' soap from alongside the basin and ran it through his hair, working up a thick lather. He ran the soap over his neck, then under his shirt to clean his armpits and chest. After using a washcloth to scrub his face, he dried off. He tied his bandanna back around his neck and slipped his vest back on. He took his badge from his pocket and pinned it to the vest. Jonas sat up and looked at him.

"You're wearing your badge? What the hell is that all about?"

"I was thinking things through on the ride down today. Decided on a change of plans."

"You'd better explain that."

"All right. There's no way in Hell we won't be spotted as lawmen the minute we reach Del Rio, not to mention we'll stand out like sore thumbs in Coffee City. Neither one of us looks even close to being Mexican, particularly you."

"Hey, hold on. I could be from one of those German families that moved to Mexico."

"Your Spanish wouldn't sound right. Your clothes ain't right, neither. In addition, this *El Atrevido* character will have driven off any other *mal hombres* who were in his territory. If they didn't leave, they disappeared permanently. He'd try'n do the same to us. Besides, I *want* him to know we're on his trail."

"You do? Why?"

"Pay attention. As I just said, *El Atrevido* will be suspicious of anyone comin' into his territory. Especially of anyone claiming to be an outlaw, even an outlaw on the run. If that man also said he'd heard of The Daring One and wanted to join up with his gang, that would make him even more suspicious. Doubly so if that man was an Anglo. You can also bet your sombrero that *El Atrevido* has spies in Del Rio, which is only about forty miles from Coffee City. I suspect he does all his raiding and robbing north and west of there. He wouldn't want to rile up the citizens of Del Rio. That just plain wouldn't be smart."

"He's probably got a lot of the Mexicans in Del Rio convinced he's out to help them, too," Jonas said.

"You can be certain of that. So we're goin' in there, then Coffee City, ridin' high, wide, and handsome, our badges in plain sight. There's bound to be a few folks who are glad to see us. With luck, even one or two who will give us information on *El Atrevido*'s habits, where he hides out, what cantinas he prefers, any women in his life. We can't count on that pretending to be just another pair of desperadoes, tryin' to make it into Mexico before the Rangers catch up to 'em. Anyone who'd like to see The Daring One taken down wouldn't confide to men whom they believe are outlaws. But they just might to a pair of Texas Rangers."

"You make some valid points, Will. And of course men who are certain the law is on their trail sometimes get careless, although we damn sure won't be that lucky. But wearin' our badges in plain sight is putting great big bull's-eyes on our backs? We might just as well be wearing signs that say 'I'm a damn son of a bitch of a Texas Ranger. Shoot me.' "

Will had to laugh.

"It's more like we'll be wearing bull's-eyes on our chests. Our nice shiny badges make an awfully tempting target for any owlhoot who'd like to put a damn bullet in us."

"Somehow that doesn't make me feel any better."

"Then look at it this way, pardner. Whether you get it from behind or from the front, you won't even know what hit you. You've been around long enough, and been in plenty of shootin' scrapes, to know that a man never hears the bullet that kills him."

"Thanks, pardner. Now I feel just fine," Jonas

retorted. "You might not hear the bullet that kills you, but you damn for certain feel it. Even a dead center shot to the head hurts when it hits, at least for a split second. And if the bastard who got you didn't aim just right, you could be hurting for a long time before the angels come to carry you across the Great Divide. I'm not hankerin' to have that happen. Not yet, anyway."

"Then you'll just have to make certain you get the damn bushwhacker before he gets you. It's simple as that."

"If you say so. I've got my doubts."

"Are you goin' to keep arguin' with me or are you goin' to clean up so we can get our supper? We can continue this discussion on the trail."

"All right."

Jonas got off the bed and washed up. It took him less than ten minutes.

"Let's go get those vittles, Will. Lead the way."

Ordinarily, most people wouldn't take much notice of Will and Jonas as they walked along the street. Neither one of them had anything outstanding enough about him to attract anyone's attention.

Will was twenty-eight, his light brown hair and brown eyes shaded by the gray Stetson he favored. He stood about five foot ten inches tall, and weighed close to one hundred ninety-five solid pounds, with broad shoulders, flat belly, and narrow hips. His clothing was plain but serviceable, a light tan shirt, brown roughout leather vest, denim trousers, scuffed brown boots, and a teal wild rag around his neck. His gun belt and holster were also plain brown leather. A Colt .45 Single Action Army "Peacemaker" revolver hung at his right hip, a Bowie knife in a brown leather sheath at his left.

Jonas had recently turned nineteen, but looked far younger. He had blond hair bleached the color of old straw where it hadn't been shaded by the tan Stetson he wore. His eyes were a deep blue. Even now, with several days' stubble of beard, he still looked more like a youth of fifteen or sixteen than a full grown man, and a full-fledged Texas Ranger to boot. That baby face often worked to his advantage, when an outlaw underestimated him in a fist or gunfight.

He was slightly shorter than Will, standing five foot eight, and a bit stockier, weighing around one hundred seventy-five pounds. His shoulders were a bit narrower than his partner's, his hips a bit broader, but his belly was flat and muscular. Like Will, his clothing was plain, but serviceable. He had on a red-checked shirt, black roughout leather vest, denim trousers, and scuffed black boots. Around his neck was a royal blue wild rag.

He wore a plain black gun belt around his waist. He had recently purchased a new .44 caliber Smith and Wesson American revolver, which he preferred over the Colts most men wore. The gun was in the holster hanging at Jonas's right hip, his Bowie knife in a sheath at his left. He wore the Smith and Wesson butt forward for a left-handed cross draw, a draw which many men swore was even faster than the conventional draw.

Most of the time when they rode into a town people assumed they were just another pair of drifting cowboys, riding the chuck line from one job to the next, moving on when the work was finished, or they got bored and needed to see what was over the horizon. Tonight, however, seeing those unmistakable silver star in silver circle badges pinned to their vests, people certainly did take notice. Most took quick, discreet glances, or whispered to their companions, while some just stared outright at the two Rangers. Some even pointed at them. While Texas Rangers wore no official uniforms or badges, more and more of them were wearing those distinctive signs of the Rangers' authority. The badges were generally hand carved from a Mexican *cinco peso* coin. Will and Jonas had had theirs made by a Mexican silversmith in Laredo.

They ignored the stares and whispers until they reached their destination, the Mid-Texas Steakhouse. A young dark-haired, dark-eyed woman greeted them when they walked in. If she noticed their badges in the dimly lit room, she didn't mention it.

"*Hablas Espanol, Senores*?"

"*Si*," Will answered.

"*Dos para cenar*?"

"*Si*."

"*Singanme por favor. Donita sera su camarera*."

"*Gracias*."

The hostess led them to a back corner table. Will and Jonas chose the two chairs which were against the back wall, where no one could get behind them, and where they had a view of the entire dining room.

"That woman has good instincts," Will said. "She knew soon as she saw our badges we'd want a table where no one could sneak up on us."

"Speaking of lawmen, look who just came through the door."

A heavyset man wearing a city marshal's badge was speaking with the hostess. She pointed at Will and Jonas.

The marshal walked over to their table. He touched two fingers to the brim of his hat when he reached it.

"Howdy, gents. I'm Mike Dolan, the San Angelo City Marshal. What brings a couple of Texas Rangers to my town? I wasn't informed any were gonna be here, and you didn't stop by my office. I'd wager you didn't stop by the Tom Green County Sheriff's Office neither. Usually the Rangers give me the courtesy of a visit when they're in town."

"Will Kirkpatrick, and my pardner, Jonas Peterson. I'm sorry we didn't stop by, Marshal, but we're only in town for the night. We simply stopped to get a hotel room for ourselves, and stalls for our horses. We're just passing through on our way to an assignment."

"I see. Do you mind telling me what that assignment is?"

"As a matter of fact, I do. It's got nothing to do with you, San Angelo, the sheriff, or Tom Green County."

Dolan's face reddened. He grew visibly angry. His voice was tight as he struggled to control his temper.

"You ain't even gonna tell me where the hell you're headed?"

"Nope."

"Why—"

Jonas cut him short.

"Marshal, if you'll excuse us, I see our waitress comin'. Me'n Will have already been on the trail for quite a few miles, and we've got plenty more miles to put behind us before we get where we're goin'. Like he already told you, we only stopped for a good night's rest before we push on. We just want to eat our meal in peace, then go back to our hotel and turn in. We're not even gonna stop by a saloon for a few drinks. It's been a real pleasure meeting you. Have a good night."

Dolan opened his mouth to say something, but thought better of it. He spluttered and walked away.

The waitress, a gray-haired woman in her early sixties, was laughing when she reached Will and Jonas's table.

"I'm your waitress, Donita. I apologize for laughing, but it's not often anyone gets Marshal Dolan's goat. Mercy sakes, it seems like you purely got under his skin."

"We didn't mean to," Will said. "He was prying into our business a little too much."

"That's our esteemed marshal, all right. Always poking his big nose where it don't belong. Of course, you can see that big belly of his coming long before his nose. That's enough about him. Would you like a menu?"

"I don't think we need one," Will said. "Bring us two of the biggest steaks you've got. Mine fried until it's almost burned, Jonas's so rare it's still mooing. Plenty of fried spuds, whatever vegetable you've got."

"That would be boiled baby carrots."

"Those will be fine. Two servings of apple crisp for dessert."

"Beverages? Beer or wine? Perhaps something stronger?"

"Just a pot of strong black coffee, thanks. We've got to get an early start come morning.

The last thing we'd need is a hangover. You want anything else, Jonas?"

Jonas shook his head.

"What you ordered sounds like plenty."

Donita smiled.

"I'll put your orders in, and be back in a jiffy with your coffee. Biscuits and gravy, too."

"Thank you," Will said.

They didn't speak until Donita was out of earshot.

"Boy howdy, that marshal sure had a helluva burr under his saddle," Jonas said. "You have any idea why?"

Will shrugged.

"*Quien sabe*? He probably likes bein' a big fish in a little pond, pushing his weight around. We hurt his pride. I wouldn't worry about him none."

"I hope I didn't speak out of turn, saying we weren't goin' to a saloon after we eat."

"Nope, you didn't. I just want to have our supper and get a good night's sleep."

"Man, I'm really stuffed," Jonas said, when they were back in their room. "That was the best, and biggest, meal I've had in a bunch of Sundays. I hope I don't break poor Rebel's back when I get on him come morning."

"Well, you didn't really have to ask for three helpings of apple crisp," Will pointed out.

"But it was so good. Almost as good as my

mother used to make. I still miss her and my pa an awful lot."

"I understand," Will said. "Let's turn in."

They undressed and climbed into bed, lying atop the sheets in the hot, stuffy room. Outside, the people on the street were beginning to head home, their noise gradually diminishing. It didn't take long for both men to fall asleep.

They were awakened some time later by the sounds of a loud argument on the boardwalk outside their room. The voices of two men arguing grew louder. There was the unmistakable sound of a fist striking flesh, then their window shattered when a man crashed through it. He landed on his back, groaned, and lay unmoving. Two bullets came through the empty window frame, to bury themselves in the opposite wall. The man's assailant ran off into the night.

Passersby shouted for assistance. One man went to find a deputy, another for a doctor. Will and Jonas jumped out of bed and grabbed their guns. Will knelt alongside the unconscious man.

"He still breathin'?" Jonas asked.

Will nodded.

"Yeah, he is. Good and steady. He's cut up some, though. It also looks like his jaw's dislocated, or mebbe busted."

"So much for our good night's sleep," Jonas complained.

"Boy howdy, you can say that again," Will answered.

A pounding came at their door.

"This is the desk clerk. Open up in there."

"Let him in, Jonas. Be careful, just in case."

"Always am."

"Sure you are."

"I'm every bit as careful as you are."

"Open up!" the clerk repeated.

"I'm comin'. Keep your shirt on."

Keeping his gun pointed at the door, Jonas stepped to the side, turned the knob, and opened the door. The clerk burst in.

"The marshal's on his way. What happened here?"

"How the hell would we know?" Jonas answered. "We heard a fight outside, then the *hombre* on the floor there came flyin' through the window. Two shots came after him, but they didn't hit anything, only put a couple of holes in your wall. Perhaps this gent thought he could get a free room for the night, I don't know."

"This isn't the time for jokes, Ranger."

"You're damn sure right it's not. Will told me this was a clean, quiet establishment. Yet we get woke up by a man crashing through the window, and gunshots besides. How the hell do you expect us to get back to sleep after all that?"

Marshal Dolan came into the room. He held a double-barreled sawed-off Greener shotgun.

"You two aren't goin' back to bed until you explain what happened here. First you claim y'all are just passing through, then the next thing I know is someone callin' for me to come quick, there's been a shooting at the Concho. Dollars to doughnuts, those damn Texas Rangers must've run a sandy by me, I said to myself. I bet they're involved somehow. Sure enough, I get here, and find you smack dab in the middle of the trouble."

"Marshal, you'd better rein in there, and hold your damn forked tongue," Will warned. "You haven't even asked if this feller lyin' here is dead or alive."

"Well, is he?"

"Is he what?"

"Dead, or alive, you damn fool."

Will stood up and fixed Dolan with an icy stare.

"He's alive, but in rough shape. Someone busted his jaw, seems like. Then they took a couple of shots at him for good measure, but it was this man's good luck they missed. You'll find the slugs in the wall right next to the door, if you care to dig them out. As far as me'n Jonas bein' involved, we had nothing whatsoever to do with whatever happened. We were both sound asleep until the yellin' and screamin' woke us up, then this man came flying through the window. Soon as this mess is cleaned up we're goin' back to bed. That's all the statement you're gonna get. You have our names from the restaurant. If you need anything more from us, send a telegram or mail a letter to Ranger Headquarters in Austin. They'll get in touch with us."

"I don't have any more rooms available," the clerk said.

"Then as soon as this man is taken away we'll stay right here. You'll be able to sweep everything up after we check out."

"But there's no window."

"We'll keep the curtains drawn. And our guns alongside us, just in case we need them."

Another man, elderly and stooped, carrying a medical bag, came in. He looked at the man on the floor, then Will and Jonas.

"I'm Doctor Horatio Parsons. What happened?"

"Someone busted or dislocated the man's jaw," Will told him. "He's pretty cut up, too. But he's breathing just fine. Strong and steady. Considering whoever did this also tried to sink a couple of bullets into him but missed, I'd say he's just fine and dandy."

Parsons knelt alongside the injured man and gave him a quick examination.

"He should be fine, but I can't do anything for him here. Marshal Dolan, would you kindly round up two or three men to carry him to my office."

"I'll get them," the clerk said.

He hurried outside, then returned with three husky men.

"Here you are, Doc."

"Thanks, Cecil. I'm obliged."

Once the injured man was removed, Dolan repeated his demands.

"Neither one of you is going anywhere until you answer my questions."

Will let out a long sigh.

"We've already told you everything we know. We have to get going right after first light. If you want to file a complaint you can do that with Headquarters. I figure you can wait until morning to dig out those bullets. Whoever attacked this man is long gone by now. You may never find him, unless the victim chooses to identify him."

"I'll have your badges."

"I doubt that."

Will turned his attention to the clerk.

"Cecil, no glass or blood got on our bed, so you don't have to worry about putting this room back together until morning. Now, if you'll excuse us, we've got to get back to catching up on our shut-eye. Good night."

"But—"

"I said *good night,* Cecil. Marshal, that goes for you, too. Take you fat butt and slide it on out of our room."

"You haven't heard the end of this, Ranger. Neither one of you has."

"I hope we have," Will retorted, "because if we haven't, I wouldn't be surprised if the state

Attorney General ordered an investigation of your office, in particular the finances. He'd send one of his investigators down here, along with a Texas Ranger or two. I'd wager they'd find some really funny things about the books. Would you care to take that chance?"

Dolan turned beet red. He opened and closed his mouth several times like a fish out of water, then turned and huffed his way out of the room.

"Well, Cecil? What are you waiting for?"

"No . . . Nothing, Ranger. No sir, nothing at all."

The clerk fled the room like a frightened rabbit.

"You gonna be able to get back to sleep, Jonas?" Will asked, closing the door. "I know damn well I sure will."

"I won't have a problem."

Jonas climbed back into his side of the bed, Will the other. Will lay on his stomach, while Jonas stretched out on his back. He lay staring at the ceiling, his hands behind his head.

"Will?"

"Yeah?"

"Did anything strike you as odd, what happened tonight?"

"You mean like you only having three helpings of dessert at supper?"

"I'm serious, Will."

Will rolled onto his side and propped himself up on one elbow, so he could look directly at

Jonas. He could see the worry in Jonas's eyes.

"All right. What've you got stuck in your craw?"

"That fight. How come it happened to take place right in front of our room? And why did one of the men just happen to come crashing through our window?"

"It was a mere coincidence, that's all. The argument probably started somewhere down the street, mebbe in a saloon, then kept escalating until it turned into a fist fight, that's all."

"I'm not satisfied that's all it was."

"Then tell me what else about it has gotten you so worked up."

"Sure. That Marshal Dolan. He sure didn't seem all that fired up about getting to the bottom of the fight. He was more interested in asking us questions. Hell, he didn't even ask if anyone knew the name of the victim."

"He probably already knew who it was."

"Then why didn't he say it when he saw the man lyin' there, out cold and all bloodied up? Or told the doctor? It would have been only natural for him to do that."

"Now you've got me starting to wonder."

"Good. Now try this on for size. The two gun-shots. Why didn't whoever pulled the trigger fire those shots into the victim outside, while he had to have still been upright? The shooter was at point blank range, so he could easily have killed the other man, yet he waited until after the other *hombre* was down on the floor in this room. That doesn't make any sense. He missed a clear chance at putting the other man down for keeps."

"Now I'm beginning to see what's got you worried. Anything else?"

"Just this. I think those bullets were meant for us. The shooter must've planned on getting us when we jumped out of bed and stood up. We were just damn lucky he missed. Sure, hitting both of us in a dark room would've been mighty difficult. But the odds of one of us catching a bullet would have been pretty good. I'm certain whoever set up this cute little scheme would have been more than happy if just one of us had been gunned down. Then it would be easier to handle the other later on."

"But the broken jaw? I doubt that was faked."

"No, it wasn't. But it could have been an accident. Either he didn't duck, or his buddy, because I'm positive they were in cahoots, forgot to pull the punch."

"Say you've got this all figured right. Who would've tried to kill us, and why?"

"My money's on Dolan."

"Why?"

"I dunno. There's just something about him. Mebbe he's working hand in glove with *El Atrevido*."

"That's kind of far-fetched. *El Atrevido*'s a

Mexican, as far as anyone knows. He sticks to the Border, where he can cross back into *manana* land if the law starts closing in on him. We're still over a hundred miles from his range."

"I'm not saying it's the best possibility. I'm just speculating. But I'm convinced that Dolan wants us out of the picture. Just can't put my finger on why."

"Jonas, I'll admit you might be onto something. But whatever it is will have to wait. We've got to stick to our orders. We'll be leaving Dolan's bailiwick in a few hours. We won't have to worry about him after that."

"Unless he sends someone ahead to ambush us, Will."

"Jonas."

"Yeah?"

"Go to sleep. You've done enough fretting for one night."

10

The first day out of San Angelo was uneventful. For quite a few miles, the trail ran alongside or close to the South Concho River. This meant for once finding water wasn't a problem. Will and Jonas camped for the night about thirty miles south of San Angelo, at a small creek which emptied into the river. There was plenty of green grass for the horses, enough to boil coffee for supper and breakfast, then fill their canteens. Once they went by the town site of Christoval the next day, they would pass the source of the South Concho. From there to Del Rio, waterholes would be few and far between.

The next afternoon found them approaching the small settlement of Sonora.

"Have you ever been there, Will?" Jonas asked.

Will shook his head.

"I can't say that I have. It wasn't established all that long ago. I'm hoping with any luck there will be a small hotel or boarding house where we can put up for the night. Because after that, there's nothin' but ninety some miles of nothin' until we reach Del Rio."

Jonas looked at Will and grinned.

"That sounds real pleasant."

Will grunted.

"You've got a mighty strange idea of what's pleasant, pard."

Sonora proved to be even less than what the Rangers had hoped. There was a combination general store/café/saloon, a few ramshackle shacks that passed for houses, and a tumbledown barn. A corral behind the barn was enclosed by a rickety fence. That fence appeared as if it would collapse if a bird landed on it, let alone contain a spooked thousand-pound horse. There was a half-filled horse trough in front of a collapsed structure. They let the horses have a short drink, then rode over to the store, dismounted, tied the horses to the sole hitching rail, where several other mounts dozed in the late afternoon sun, idly switching their tails at pestering flies, and went inside.

No one was in the store except a skinny, tow-headed boy of about twelve. They nodded a greeting to him as they walked through the store to the adjoining room, which held the café and bar. Five men stood at the bar, two more were sitting at a table, working on sandwiches and playing a two-handed game of poker. A man and woman stood behind the bar, he cleaning glasses, she engaged in idle talk with the customers. They were both in their early forties, he dark-haired, with a thick moustache, she a redhead with green eyes and a full figure.

"Howdy, gents," the bartender called when he saw them. He glanced at the badges pinned to their vests.

"Texas Rangers, huh?"

"Yep," Will answered.

"What brings the Rangers to a sleepy town like this place?"

"We're just passing through," Will answered. "Sonora seems like as good a place as any in these parts to spend the night."

The bartender grinned.

"Well, as I'm sure you must have noticed, of course it's the only place within forty miles in any direction to spend the night. So you made the right choice."

Everyone in the room laughed, as if on cue. It was obvious they'd heard that same joke who knew how many times before.

"I reckon," Will said.

"Welcome. I'm Bob Adams, and this is my wife, Suzanne. What can we get for y'all?"

"My handle's Will. My pardner's is Jonas. We're looking for a meal, but first, is there any place in town where we can spend the night? And a stable to put up our horses?"

"Your pard don't talk much, does he?"

"Oh, he can yammer up a storm. That's why I try not to let him get started."

"I save my words up until they're needed," Jonas said.

“More folks should do that,” one of the customers said.

“You’re right, Scully. Why don’t you start doin’ that right here and now?” Adams said.

He turned back to Will and Jonas.

“There’s really nothing you could call a hotel. We had one, but if you came in from the north, you saw what’s left of it. A tornado took it down a few years back. That twister killed Jace Barker, the owner, his wife Janice, and five folks who were stayin’ there.”

“We saw it when we let our horses have a drink at the trough,” Jonas said.

“There’s no one with rooms to let, neither,” Adams continued. “However, you’re welcome to bed down in the old livery stable if that suits you. Or the two houses either side of it. They’re all three abandoned. There is a pump in the barn that still works, and a couple of buckets, so you can water your horses.”

“We’ll check them out,” Will said. “If worse comes to worst we can always unroll our blankets and sleep outside. Do you happen to have any hay or grain for sale? Our horses are mighty gaunted from bein’ pushed hard the past several days.”

“Our boy Jamie’s in the store,” Suzanne answered. “He’ll get what you need.”

“We’re obliged.”

“Will, how about ordering some grub for us?” Jonas said. “I’m gonna dry up and blow away in the next strong breeze if I don't get some food in my belly soon."

"Y'all will have to forgive my pardner for bein' rude," Will said. "He gets ornery when he's hungry. And he's always hungry."

"We've got venison stew on the menu tonight," Suzanne said. "Jamie shot a mule deer three days back, so the meat's fresh. Stew's chock full of that, plus potatoes, carrots, and onions. I baked bread and churned butter this morning to go along with the stew. And baked a dried peach pie for dessert."

"That does sound good," Jonas said. "I'll take a double order."

"I'll have the same, but just regular sized," Will added.

"I'll bring it right out. Choose any table you'd like."

"How about something to cut the dust from your throats to go along with that?" Adams asked.

"You have beer?" Will said.

"Of course I have beer. It's even cold. I get ice shipped down from San Angelo in the winter, put it in the root cellar, and cover it with a thick layer of sawdust. It lasts most near all summer."

"Then we'll have two to start," Will ordered.

They took a table near the back wall. Suzanne brought out their meals and placed the food in front of them.

"If y'all need anything else, just let me know," she said. "I'll bring the pie soon as you're ready for it."

"This looks like plenty," Will said. "Looks and smells delicious, too. Thank you."

"You're welcome."

Suzanne gave Will a wink and smile, a smile that hinted venison stew was not the only dish on the menu, if he so desired. He blushed.

Will and Jonas ate until they could eat no more. They pushed back from the table.

"You boys are all finished?" Suzanne asked.

"We sure are," Jonas said. "I'm so stuffed I'm afraid if I ate another bite the buttons on my denims would explode, fly across the room, and take someone's eye out. That would be plumb embarrassing. Particularly if my pants busted open and fell down."

Suzanne giggled, but didn't bat an eyelash.

"How about a few drinks before you call it a night?" Adams asked, from behind the bar.

"We might just come back for some, but right now we need to get the feed for our horses, settle them, and decide where we're gonna bed down for the night," Will answered.

"We're generally here until ten," Adams said. "There's not much call to stay any later than that. The store closes at six. Jamie will get you whatever supplies you require."

"We're obliged," Will said.

He and Jonas went into the store. Jamie was half-heartedly sweeping the floor.

"Howdy, son," Will said. "Your pa told us you'd get the supplies we need."

"Howdy yourself," Jamie answered, with a grin. "I'll be happy to. Anything's better than chasing the dust around this place. It's a waste of time. It'll only be back by tomorrow afternoon. What can I get you fellers?"

"Enough oats for our horses for tonight and the next two days," Will requested. "Also some hay. Would you be able to bring the hay over to the old stable for us?"

"Sure. I'll tote whatever you purchase over there for you. Any supplies for yourselves?"

"Five pounds of bacon, and a sack of beans."

Jamie lowered his voice when he asked his next question.

"You fellers are Rangers, right?"

"Yes, we are," Jonas answered.

Jamie's next question was spoken in a whisper.

"Are you certain you've got enough ammunition?"

Will kept his voice down when he answered.

"We've got plenty of extra shells. Why?"

"You might need them before you leave this here town."

"Why?"

"I've said too much already. Just please be

careful. And don't sleep too sound. I'll bring over more cartridges. Forty-fours and .45s for your six-guns. Shells for your rifles, too. You don't mind if I add those to your bill?"

"Won't that get you in trouble with your pa, even if we do pay for the ammunition?"

"He ain't my pa. And Suzanne ain't my ma. My folks died of cholera. I don't have any other kin, so I had to take a job here or plumb starve to death. Bob fleeces travelers out of every cent he can. Suzanne's just a whore who claims to be his wife. Even took his last name. They're both real bad. Did you have any whiskey yet?"

"No," Will said. "Would that be a mistake?"

"It sure would. Bob puts something in the drinks, if he's decided an *hombre* is a good target. Listen, that's enough talkin'. Bob or Suzanne will get suspicious if you're here too long. I'll hide the ammunition in the grain bag."

"Don't risk getting in trouble on our account, son," Jonas said. "We can handle ourselves."

"Not if you don't know what you're up against, you can't."

Jamie raised his voice.

"That will be a total of $8.75. I'll wrap up your order and have it to you in a jiffy."

"We're obliged," Will said.

He handed Jamie a gold eagle.

"Ten dollars," Jamie said. "I'll get your change."

“No. Keep the change to buy yourself something nice,” Will said.

“Gee willikers! Thank you, Mister Ranger Sir. Thank you.”

“You’re welcome. We’ll be at the old stable caring for our horses. Don’t forget our receipt. We need that to be reimbursed by Austin. See you in a few minutes.”

Will and Jonas went to their horses.

“Will, what in the blue blazes do you think that boy meant?” Jonas asked, as he untied Rebel’s reins and swung into the saddle.

Will shrugged as he got onto Pete. He and Jonas started for the stable.

“I dunno, except he sure as hell was warning us to watch out. I’m betting Bob and his wife set up travelers to be robbed. Since they wouldn’t want any witnesses, they probably kill their victims and dispose of the bodies.”

“Wouldn’t someone report those *hombres muertos* missing?”

“I’d imagine our charming host and hostess pick their victims carefully. They choose men who are alone or in pairs. Most likely quiz them about their backgrounds to find out about friends or kinfolk. That wouldn’t matter much anyway. You’re well aware how easy it is for a person to just disappear and never be seen again in this God-forsaken territory. If anyone comes snooping around and asking questions, the only answer they'd get would be the missing person never came through here."

"Do you think they'd try anything stupid, knowing we're Rangers?"

"I wouldn't have thought so, but that boy sure believes they will. So we'll take his advice. It's also possible they believe we're onto them, or at least are suspicious, and think we have come here to do some snooping around. That means they have to get rid of us. It looks like we won't get much sleep tonight after all."

"If the Adamses and some of their friends, or some other bunch of no-goods, are gonna try for us, they most likely won't make their move until they think we're asleep. So we'll have to fool them into thinking we are."

"You've got a good point, Jonas. Unless I see something to change my mind, we'll probably be safest in the barn. We passed those houses Adams mentioned on the way into town. They looked about ready to collapse at any time. A good stiff breeze could bring them tumblin' down around our ears. The stable's also in rough shape, but it should have sturdier framework. Also more places to take cover, wait, and pick off whoever's after our hides."

"We'll have to make certain we find a good place inside it to keep our horses safe from flyin' lead. As best we can, anyway."

"I've been pondering on that already. It seems

like great minds think alike there, pardner."

"Or we've been ridin' together for so long we can each guess what the other one's thinking, like an old married couple. Will, if that's the case, I ain't gonna be the wife. Not on your life, pal. You can bet your hat and everything underneath it on that."

Will laughed.

"A visit to one of the sporting houses in Del Rio will get you rid of that notion."

"Yeah. *If* we live long enough to get there."

"That's true. Well, here we are. Let's get inside and take a look around."

They rode into the barn and dismounted.

"Sorry, big feller," Will apologized to Pete. "I'll get the gear off you, feed you, and rub you down, but then the saddle and bridle go right back on. We might have to light a shuck outta here right quick."

"The same goes for you, Rebel," Jonas said. "So I don't want any complaints, ya jughead."

"Let's put Pete and Rebel into the center stalls," Will suggested. "Any bullets that punch through the walls would be too spent to hurt them, if they even traveled that far."

"Across from each other, or next to each other?" Jonas asked.

"I'd say next to each other. Neither one of 'em's afraid of gunfire, but they'd still be happier closer together."

"That makes sense. Let's give them a good currying while we're waiting for Jamie to show up with their feed. I damn sure hope he knows what he's doin', and doesn't get caught."

"You can say that again."

They had just taken the gear off their horses and begun grooming them when they heard footsteps outside.

"That must be Jamie," Jonas said. Nonetheless, he gripped the butt of his American, ready to pull the gun from its holster and put it into action at the first sign of trouble.

"Rangers, are you in there?"

"That's Jamie all right," Will said. "Let's meet him at the door, just in case he's got some friends with him."

"We'll be right there, son," he called.

"Do you think that young'n might be setting us up?" Jonas asked.

Will shook his head.

"*Quien sabe*? I doubt it, but there's no use in taking unnecessary risks. That's how a man winds up dead."

Jamie was waiting where the door to the barn had once been. That missing door was both an advantage and disadvantage for the Rangers. It allowed any potential attackers clear shots into the main aisle. It also provided them a way to rush anyone inside the barn a clear pathway, without the necessity of battering down the door to gain access. On the other hand, anyone inside, such as Will and Jonas, could take cover behind the thick board walls of the individual stalls and cut down anyone who came into view. A group of men attempting to rush the barn would pay a high price indeed before overpowering the Rangers.

"I've got your goods, Rangers," Jamie said. "I left them just inside the doorway. Mr. Adams said to thank you again for your order. Mrs. Adams says she hopes you'll stop by again soon."

"Tell them they're welcome. We might stop by on our way back," Will said. "We just have no idea when that will be."

"Or even if," Jonas added. "We never know where we'll be sent next."

"I'll let them know. I'd better get back to the store in case any more customers come along. The extra items are in the feed sack. I hope you'll make good use of them."

"I'm certain we will. Good night, Jamie."

"G'night, Rangers."

"Time to feed the horses," Will said.

Pete and Rebel were nickering for their supper. The nickers became louder and more pleading when they saw their riders approaching with grain and hay.

"Simmer down. You're not that hungry," Will scolded Pete.

He set down the sack of grain and opened it. He whistled when he saw its contents.

"What have you got there, Will?" Jonas asked.

Will reached into the sack and pulled out six boxes of cartridges, two of .45s, two of .44s, and two of .44-40s.

"Whoo-ee. That kid must expect we're gonna be up against an army," Jonas exclaimed. "He's downright smart, too. He noticed your gun's a .45 caliber, and mine's a .44. He must have taken a look at our weapons while we were having supper."

"Here's a note."

"Read it."

"It's kind of hard to make out his writing. His spelling's not all that good either. I'll do my best."

Will squinted to decipher the hastily scribbled writing in the dim light of the barn.

Rangers. I sawr Mr. Adams talkin' reel quiet-like with some of the men in the salloon. Herd a litle. Seams like they was makin' plans for tonite. Hope this is enuff warnning.

"Boy howdy. The boy took an awful chance getting this note to us," Jonas said. "If he's right, we're in for one helluva fight."

"If he's right, and we come outta the fight alive, we'll have to somehow get him away from here. His life won't be worth a plugged nickel."

"That's for sure," Jonas agreed. "What we do with him will have to wait until after we get through tonight. *If* we manage to do that without gettin' shot so full of holes we'll look like sieves."

"Let's get the horses fed before they have a nervous breakdown," Will said. "After that we'll look around this barn and figure out the best way to hold off any raiders."

"Yeah, we filled our bellies, so I reckon they deserve to eat, too."

"Good thing we did, or we'd be facing whatever we're up against on empty stomachs."

"You forget it's also a damn good thing we didn't stay around for some drinks after supper, from what Jamie suspects."

Once the horses were cared for, munching hay in their stalls, Will and Jonas went through the barn.

"At least the back door's still in place," Jonas said. "That means it'll be harder for Adams and his bunch to come at us from both sides. That does make it easier for them to get closer without us knowing it, though."

"That also makes it really easy to sneak up and fire this place," Will answered. "This stable's a tinderbox. It'll burn fast and hot. If they do manage to set it on fire, the only chance we'll have is to ride outta here like hell, shooting, and hope we can break through before they cut us down."

"If that happens, you can bet your boots they'll try'n get Pete and Rebel first. Once they were down, we'd be sittin' ducks."

"That's provided we were lucky enough not to break our necks or get knocked senseless when we hit the ground. And if our horses didn't land on top of us. Listen, we don't know how much time we have to get ready. Let's go through this place and see where the best defensive positions are at."

Will and Jonas did a walkthrough of the barn. When they were finished, they realized the odds of holding off any attackers were far less than they'd hoped.

"These walls have so many holes and rotten boards they couldn't even stop a moth, let alone a bullet," Jonas said.

"We'd better hope a damn moth doesn't land on the roof. If one does, the whole place is liable to collapse," Will answered. "It's a damn shame we can't use the hayloft, but it's barely hanging on. And the ladder's long gone."

"If Adams does come after us, how many men do you think he'll have with him?"

"I dunno. I'm thinking it will be some or all of the men who were in the saloon tonight. There were seven, then Adams himself, so that makes eight all together. That's just speculation. Some of those *hombres* might not be in cahoots with Adams. But there might be others who are. We'll just have to wait and see."

"Maybe Jamie was wrong, and nothing will happen. He just might've made up the entire tale to talk us into helping him get away from here. He might have hoped we'd just fall for it, and take him with us."

"If nothing happens, that would be the best case scenario," Will said. "I don't think Jamie was lying, though. He seemed real scared, for one. For two, he took an awfully big risk sneaking the extra ammunition to us. I'd wager the boy's on the level."

"So we just wait and see what happens."

"We just wait and see what happens."

Jonas shook his head.

"No matter how many or few men Adams has, we're still in a bad situation. They can wait us out, burn us out, or just pump so many bullets into this barn at least some of them are bound to make a hit. The only positive thing I can come up with is we've got plenty of ammunition, thanks to Jamie. If those sons of bitches do manage to get us, they'll pay a helluva high price. We'll take as many of them with us as we can."

"That's damn wishful thinking, Jonas."

"I know, Will. But right now that's about all I've got."

"You've got your six-gun and rifle to go along with that wishful thinking," Will pointed out. "If we can get a few of them right off, the rest just might turn tail and run."

Jonas gave a rueful smile.

"Now who's doin' some wishful thinking, pardner?"

"I'll be doin' some serious praying, too. We'd better get ready. I'm guessing they'll attack from both ends of the barn. That means we'll have to split up. Once the attack starts, we can change positions as necessary. You want the front or the back?"

"It doesn't matter to me."

"Me, neither. Why don't we flip a coin? You call it."

"That's fair."

Will dug in his pocket and removed a quarter.

"You call it. If it's heads you take the front, tails the back. Ready?"

"Ready."

Will tossed the quarter into the air.

"Heads," Jonas called.

Will grabbed the coin as it fell and slapped it onto the back of his left hand.

"It's tails."

"Reckon I'd better get back there. It'll be harder to spot anyone sneaking up on us, but I'll have more cover than you will. Good luck, and give a shout if you hear or see anything. And don't fall asleep. That's what they're counting on."

"The same goes for you, Jonas."

It was about two in the morning when Will saw a group of men carrying rifles walking toward the barn, staying close to the buildings and in the shadows as much as possible. The moon was new, so the only illumination was the dim light of the stars, making it difficult to pick out objects or persons.

Will picked up his Winchester and called to his partner.

"Jonas, it looks like they're coming. Get ready."

"All right. How many?"

"They're still too far away for me to tell. I'd guess a half dozen at least. Hold on. They're splitting up. It seems we guessed right. They're gonna come at us from at least two sides."

"Are you planning on givin' 'em a warning?"

"Not until they're well within range. We need to hold off any shootin' until we're certain they're after us. Then one warning shot into the dirt right in front of 'em. If they keep on a-comin', we'll get as many of them as we can, and hope it scares off the rest. If not, we just keep fighting and pray we come out on top."

"All right."

Will lay on his belly in the middle of the aisle, where he would not be silhouetted, and was mostly hidden inside the dark barn. Jonas poked his rifle through a wide crack in the back door, from which he had a good view of anyone approaching.

Time seemed to stop as they waited. Muscles grew tense, nerves on edge. Sweat beaded on their foreheads, ran down their backs and chests, plastering their shirts to their flesh, making large wet circles under their armpits. The waiting was especially hard on Jonas, knowing he had to hold back until Will made the first move. He jumped when Will's rifle cracked, followed by him shouting at the oncoming men.

"Hold it right there!" Will ordered. "If any of you takes one more step that man will get a rifle slug clean through his guts. If you're peaceable, drop your weapons and get your hands in the air."

"What're you on the prod for, Ranger? This is Bob Adams. Me and my friends are just coming to check on you and your pardner. We want to make certain you're all comfy and cozy, and getting a good night's sleep."

"At this hour of the morning? Carrying guns, sneaking up on us, keepin' to the shadows?"

"It's damn dark out here. What the hell makes you think we were sneaking up on you?"

Jonas could hear the conversation.

"Will, he's just tryin' to buy time while the others get around back here," he muttered to himself. "Quit his stalling and let him have it if he doesn't give up right now."

A shadowy figure came into Jonas's view, racing for the back of the barn.

"The hell with this. The time for talking is over," Jonas said. He lifted his Winchester to his shoulder, took aim, and fired. The bullet hit his target in the chest. The man stumbled, pitched forward into the corral fence. The rotten boards collapsed from the impact. The man landed face down in a jumble of splintered wood. He never moved again.

Four men who'd been following the first raced for cover after seeing their partner go down. Jonas shot one of them in mid-air as he attempted to jump over a woodpile. The man landed hard atop the logs, then rolled behind them.

"That's two out of the fight anyway, although I'm not certain how bad the second one is hit."

Jonas dove to the floor when a hail of bullets hit the back door, sending splinters flying. Several of the lead slugs punched through the boards, whining over the prone Ranger.

Gunfire had erupted at the front of the barn.

I wonder if Will's gonna be able to stop those sons of bitches before they get to him.

That was the only thought Jonas had time for, as the besiegers raked the barn with almost continuous gunfire. When it fell silent, Jonas peered through one of the newly opened cracks in the wall. Behind the woodpile where the man he'd shot had fallen, he could see the sudden flash of a match being struck, then the brighter glow of a flame.

Dollars to doughnuts those bastards are gonna try and set this old barn aflame. That's what I'd do if the situation was reversed. They're hopin' they've already nailed me, and killed me dead. Soon as that hombre *starts runnin' with a torch, they'll open up again to keep me pinned down. They ain't gonna take the chance I might start shootin' back.*

While Jonas was trying to hold off the men at the rear, Will had his own problems on the street side. Seven men had rushed his position. He put a rifle bullet through one's belly, causing the man to fold in half, then go into a head over heels roll before he lay still. He got a second one in the chest, then a bullet tore along the left side of his head, leaving him stunned. He rolled up against a partition, lying there breathing heavily and waiting for the dizziness to subside. He could hear the gunfire from the back of the barn, the crack of Jonas's rifle, the muffled sound of the shots fired by the men outside.

Will knew he was in trouble. He'd been wounded, how seriously he couldn't tell. The injury might just be a deep bullet graze, or a concussion, perhaps even a skull fracture. He'd shot down two men, but that still left him outnumbered five to one. He had no idea how Jonas was faring, except that since the gunfire continued, his partner was still alive. How long either of them would be able to hold out was the big question, for which there was no answer.

• • •

Jonas took a desperate chance. He got back up and knocked out one of the boards protecting him. That gave him a better view of the attackers and a wider field of fire.

"C'mon if you're comin', you damned sons of bitches."

One of the men rose from behind the woodpile, carrying the torch. He started toward the barn, not running, but staggering, weaving, and stumbling as he came.

"There's somethin' not right about that *hombre.* What in the blue blazes is he doin'? It looks like he's drunk. Somethin' about him doesn't look right, either. He's kind of slumped over, like he has to see where he's puttin' his feet down."

As the man drew nearer, Jonas squinted to get a better look. Instead of just one, there appeared to be two men, one holding the torch, the other in front of him.

"You no good bastards!"

Jonas realized one of the men, the one in front, was either dead or unconscious.

"That must be the *hombre* I shot. The other one's using him as a shield against any bullets I throw at him. Well, lemme take care of that."

Jonas came to his feet, took careful aim, and opened fire. He purposely shot low, aiming at the dead man's belly, where there were no large bones to stop the bullets as they ripped through his guts, passed between or shattered his back ribs, and tore into the man propping him up. He levered and fired as quickly as he could, emptying his rifle into the approaching men.

His plan worked. The torch bearer screamed when several of Jonas's bullets passed through the first man and plowed into his belly and groin. He let go of his human shield, then fell on top of him, dropping the torch when he collapsed. The burning firebrand landed on his back, flickered for an instant, then flared up as it took hold of the dead man's shirt. The flames grew rapidly, smoke rising into the night sky. Soon the acrid stench of burning fabric and human flesh filled the air.

Jonas dropped his rifle and pulled his Smith and Wesson from its holster. He kicked open the barn door.

"All right, you damned sons of bitches. If you want me, here I am. Come and get me. But you'd better be prepared to die and meet the devil, because I won't go down easy."

Thinking they had an easy target, the remaining two men came out of cover, shooting. Jonas returned their fire, zigzagging as he ran toward them. He made a final lunge, then dove to the dirt, shooting as he slid behind the still burning bodies of the torch bearer and his partner. He shot down both men with bullets in each one's chest.

"Y'all just made a helluva mistake, and it damn

for certain cost you," Jonas shouted. "Now to go lend Will a hand."

Jonas punched out the empty cartridges and reloaded his six-gun, then got up and hurried to help his partner.

Will had rolled back onto his belly, and was firing from his prone position. However, he had no real cover, and the muzzle flashes from his rifle exposed his position. He nailed one man in the head, dropping him as if he were pole-axed, then rolled to his left, knowing he had only a fifty-fifty chance of being correct, but also aware that most men tended to shoot to the right at an unseen, moving target. If he'd guessed wrong, and even one of the men chose to shoot left, then a bullet in his head would bring an end to his Ranger career . . . and his life.

He turned when he heard footsteps approaching from behind, thinking Jonas had been gunned down and he was now caught between both groups.

"Don't shoot, Will! It's Jonas. I'm gonna lend you a hand."

He took cover behind a support post.

"What in hell took you so damn long?" Will asked.

"I was a mite busy coverin' your back, pard. How many men are left out there?"

"I think four, but I can't be certain."

Jonas took a snap shot. Luck was with him.

His bullet took a man in the stomach. Will put a finishing slug into his chest.

"Make that three, Will."

More shots rang out from the street. Two of the remaining three would-be ambushers went down with bullets in their backs. The last one turned and shot at the source of the new gunfire. Someone cried out in pain. Will and Jonas each put a bullet into the final bushwhacker's back. Silence descended on Sonora, broken only by the moans of the mysterious gunman.

"What the hell just happened?" Jonas exclaimed.

"I'm not certain, but we'd better find out right quick, before any reinforcements show up," Will answered.

They reloaded their pistols before leaving the barn. Walking across the street, they followed the pained cries of the wounded man who had most likely saved their lives, checking each of the men lying in the street on the way. All were dead. With a bit of help from an unexpected and still unknown ally, the Rangers had beaten the long odds against them. They were survivors, at least for this night.

The wounded man was lying curled up on his side. Jonas rolled him onto his back.

"Jamie!"

"Ranger. Reckon I'm . . . done for. But I had to . . . take a hand. I knew the two of you could . . . never outgun . . . Adams and his men. You were

. . . the only chance I had to . . . break free from . . . Adams. Had to . . . try'n help you . . . me, too."

Will knelt alongside the boy.

"Hush. Keep quiet and rest. Let me check and see how hard you've been hit."

The right side of Jamie's shirt was blood soaked. Will opened it to reveal a deep bullet furrow between two of the boy's ribs. He took off his neckerchief and stuffed it into the wound to stanch the flow of blood.

"How bad is it?" Jonas asked.

Will shook his head. "I can't tell. It looks like the slug's still in him. How bad it is depends on how deep it penetrated. Jamie, you might be all right, but we have to get you to a doctor, *pronto*. Is there one in this town?"

"N . . . no. Mrs. Adams took care . . . of folks who got sick . . . or hurt. Not without . . . money up front, though."

Will looked up at Jonas.

"What do you think?"

"I think we're caught between the devil and the deep blue sea, that's what I think. We'd be takin' one helluva chance bringing Jamie to Suzanne Adams. Her so-called husband's lyin' dead over there with our bullets in him. So are a bunch of her friends. Once she knows that, she'll most likely make certain to kill this boy. Us, too. She must have more friends who'd be more than happy to help her with that little chore. But it's a two-day ride back to San Angelo, three to Del Rio. If you can at least patch him up some, will Jamie be able to ride that far?"

"I could try, but it'd be touch and go. There is the possibility we could find help at a ranch along the way. I know one thing, though. Whatever decision we make, we've gotta make it damn quick. It won't be long until Suzanne figures out something went wrong. We need to *vamoose*."

"Ranger, do I get a say in this?" Jamie asked.

"I guess you should, since we're talking about your life," Will answered.

"I'd rather take my . . . chances of dyin' along the trail than facing . . . Suzanne. She's always . . . hated me, ever since she told me she wanted to . . . teach me about making love. When I said no, she . . . she forced herself on me. I've felt dirty and ashamed ever since. The only reason I ain't dead . . . already is Bob wanted to keep me as his slave, for lack . . . of a better word. With him gone, she'd be sure . . . to kill me."

"Then we'd better get a move on," Will said. "Jonas, do you think you can scare up another horse?"

"It'd be awful risky. Rebel will carry double. Jamie won't be able to stay on a horse for very far anyway. It'll be better to have him riding behind me on my horse, so he can hang onto me. It'll be slow goin', but we won't need to travel the rest of the night anyway, only far enough to hole up until daylight."

"That makes sense," Will agreed. "Jamie, I've got to tear your shirt up to pad the wound, and also tie the bandages in place. I'll do that while Jonas gets the horses."

"I appreciate . . . that, Ranger. The sooner we're . . . shut of this town the better."

Within fifteen minutes, Jamie's wound was bandaged, and they were riding south, leaving the bodies of their attackers scattered in the street.

Suzanne Adams wasted no time on grieving her late husband, or any of his partners. The bodies were buried at dawn, the gravediggers paid off in whiskey, and by nine o'clock the store, café, and saloon were open under her proprietorship. Within two weeks, the time it took her to bring down some girls from San Angelo, she would add a small brothel to her business enterprises.

11

Unaware that Suzanne wasn't upset one bit about losing her husband and the others, Will and Jonas rode south about fifteen miles, stopping in a grove of scrub oak and mesquite about two hours before sunup. They would be well hidden in the thick underbrush.

Jamie slid off Rebel's back and stumbled to one of the oaks, sitting down with his back against its trunk.

Will and Jonas quickly dismounted.

"Are you still hanging on, Jamie?" Will asked.

"Yeah. Sort of. I just feel awfully weak and tired."

"That's to be expected. I'll check you soon as we get the saddles off the horses."

"Will, you go ahead and do that now," Jonas said. "I'll take care of the horses. I'll let them have some grain once they've cooled down."

"That'd be a real help," Will said. He went over to Jamie.

"Let me have a look at your wound. Once I remove the bandages, lie down, and roll over onto your left side."

Jamie complied, grunting when pain shot through his ribs.

As best he could in the dim light, Will examined

the young boy's injury. He pressed against his lower back, where he believed the bullet had lodged.

Jamie jerked and yelped.

"What the hell are you tryin' to do to me, Ranger? Finish me off?"

"I have to try and figure out if the bullet is pressing against any vital organ, or has shifted around inside you. So far, it doesn't seem to have done either. It also appears the bleeding has mostly stopped, which is damn good news. I'd sure hate to see you bleed out. Soon as it's light enough I'll take a better look, then replace the bandages. You try and get some sleep until then. We'll rest here for a few hours, since we're all bushed."

"Ain't you worried about anyone from Sonora hunting us, Ranger? It seems to me we're in no shape to fight 'em off if they catch up to us."

"It will take a while to organize a posse to come after us. We're pretty well hidden among these trees," Will assured him. "But mainly the horses need rest as much, or more, than we do. We pushed them as hard as we dared with Rebel carrying double. Also, as long as you're riding with us, you might as well start using our names. It's Will or Jonas, not Ranger. Deal?"

"Deal."

"Good. You just take it easy while I go help Jonas with the horses. Try and sleep. We don't dare make a fire, because anyone passing by would be certain to see it. I'll get a blanket for you in case you get a chill."

"*Gracias*. I'm obliged . . . Will."

"*Por nada.* You saved our bacon with the warning and the extra ammunition. With any luck, we'll come across a farm or ranch today where we can find someone to help remove the bullet."

"Will, I just realized you've been hurt, too. It looks like a bullet came awful close to blowing your brains out. I'm sorry for making you worry about me when you've been hurt yourself."

"I'm not hurt that bad. After I clean out the wound I'll be good as new. You try and get that sleep. Tomorrow we've got to put a lot more miles behind us."

Will got a blanket from his bedroll and covered Jamie with it, then joined Jonas, who was just pouring some oats on the ground, two piles far enough apart Pete and Rebel wouldn't fight over their meal.

"How's the boy doing?" Jonas asked.

"Better than I expected, but I can't say for certain what'll happen to him if that bullet isn't removed, and soon. It doesn't seem to have hit any of his vitals, at least not so far, but riding on the back of a horse could jar it enough it might move. I'm no doctor, but it seems to be lodged close to, maybe even pressing on, his kidney."

"That's not good."

"Nope. He's also lost an awful lot of blood. Right now the bleeding seems to have stopped, or almost, so I don't have to tell you bouncing around, even if we keep the horses to a walk while we try'n get Jamie to a doctor, could start him bleeding all over again. That would most likely kill him. He hasn't developed a fever yet, so that's one good sign."

"So would blood poisoning, which is a real risk. Speaking of blood poisoning, when do you intend to tell me about that bullet graze on your thick skull? You think I didn't notice it? It looks pretty deep. I was more worried about Jamie than you so I was waitin' until we stopped to ask you about it. Now that I've had a closer look, it needs tending to."

"It is deep. Knocked me silly when I took that slug. You, and then Jamie, came along in the nick of time. I'll wash it out and wrap a bandage around my head. That'll take care of it."

"You'd better hope so. I dunno about you, but I'm plumb tuckered out. Let's turn in. I'd also suggest we sleep in a little, unless you or Jamie take a turn for the worse."

"That sounds like a dang fine idea. I'll take one more quick look at Jamie, then we'll call it a day . . . or a night."

"Call it whatever you want, it's been one helluva time since we rode into Sonora. And we've still got three days to Del Rio. And a wounded young'n on our hands. And one Ranger who'll feel like he's got the worst hangover of his life when he wakes up. Much more of this Ranger life and Huntsville will start looking like Paradise in comparison."

"You're such a cheerful cuss. Why don't you just shut up and get to bed. Soon as I look in on Jamie I'll be right along."

"That sounds reasonable to me."

Jamie had fallen into a deep sleep, so Will didn't disturb him. Jonas was a few yards away, already under his blanket and snoring.

Will took the time to clean out and bandage his head wound, then he also slid under his blanket. As exhausted as his partner, plus with his wound now throbbing, Will was asleep within five minutes after his head hit the saddle he was using for a pillow.

12

Despite their intention to sleep late, force of habit found Will and Jonas awake before the sun was an hour above the eastern horizon. With no sign of pursuit, they decided to build a fire and cook breakfast. All three needed nourishment, Will and Jamie in particular to help build strength and fight off the effects of their wounds.

Jamie was still asleep. He awakened at the mouth-watering aromas of bacon sizzling in the pan, coffee boiling, and biscuits rising.

He yawned and stretched, giving a soft cry when he got a stitch in his side.

"It's about time you woke up, lazy bones," Will said, grinning. "I thought you were gonna sleep the day away. Are you still feeling all right?"

"No, I'm feeling like a man who's been shot. How's *your* head?"

For one of the few times in his life, Will was too surprised to make a snappy retort.

"It seems he's feeling feisty, Will," Jonas said, suppressing a laugh. "That's a good sign. Jamie, if you're hungry, breakfast will be ready in a few minutes."

"I'm hungry all right, but I need to take a leak more."

"There's plenty of bushes to choose from," Will said. "Take it easy when you try'n stand up. You might get a bit dizzy. I'll see if I can do anything about the bullet you're totin' after we eat. I probably won't be able to do much except clean the hole in your side. I've got to try and keep you from developing an infection until we reach someplace where we can find help."

"I can live with that. At least the damn slug ain't stuck in my belly. If it was, I wouldn't be one bit hungry."

Jamie got slowly to his feet and wandered into the brush. Jonas watched him until he was out of sight.

"What're we gonna do with him, Will? It'd be difficult taking him all the way to Del Rio. Yet I don't see any other choice. There's not one settlement between here and Del Rio."

"Tell me something I don't already know. There's bound to be some ranches or farms we'll pass by. I'm hoping we can get help for Jamie at one of them. With luck even leave him at one until he's recovered. Then he can decide what he wants to do."

"He's only a young'n, Will. Whatever happens, we have to make certain he's not put right back into a situation like he was in Sonora. You know what happened to me. The same could happen to Jamie."

"One thing's for certain," Will said. "We have to find somewhere for him before we take on *El Atrevido* and his gang."

"Yeah. I reckon that's the thanks we get for doin' our job too well," Jonas said. "We get a good jump on cleaning up the territory around Sweetwater, so we get sent to the Border to try'n run down one of the worst Mexican *bandidos* to ever plague Texas."

Jamie emerged from the brush.

"I'm back, and I'm plumb starved. Is breakfast almost ready?"

"It is," Will answered. "You get the chore of cleaning the dishes after we eat."

"Aww. Do I have to?"

"Would you rather ride all day on an empty belly?"

Jamie signed.

"I'll do the dishes."

"You made the right decision."

After their meal, Will checked Jamie's wound. It was hot to the touch, but there was no sign of a spreading infection, at least not yet. However, if they couldn't find someone to locate and dig out the bullet before much more time passed, infection, then gangrene and death, was inevitable. Riding on the back of a horse might also cause the bullet to shift to where it was pressing on a vital organ. The most urgent business of the day would be finding help for the boy.

Once Will cleaned out and rebandaged his own wound again, they broke camp and now, two days north of Del Rio, resumed their journey. They passed a number of small ranches en route, each of which offered them water and a chance to rest, none able to treat Jamie or take him in while he recuperated.

Just before sundown, they had traveled a little over thirty miles. They were approaching a homestead which appeared larger than most in the region.

"Do you reckon we can get some supper and mebbe be allowed to bunk down for the night at that place over yonder, Will?" Jonas asked. "Jamie can't go much farther. He fell asleep a few miles back. Stuck his hands behind my gun belt to keep him from fallin' off Rebel."

"I damn sure hope so," Will answered. "I'm pretty well bushed myself. My headache ain't getting any better either. Our horses are plumb worn out, too. Though I am wondering why there doesn't seem to be anyone about the place."

They rode into the ranch yard. A woman in her early fifties, with brown hair starting to gray, and piercing brown eyes, holding a Remington double-barreled shotgun, opened the front door. She stood just inside it, eyeing the newcomers with suspicion.

"You boys state your business. If you're lookin' to stir up trouble, you've come to the right place. I know how to handle it. Try anything, and you'll both get bellies full of buckshot."

Will and Jonas raised their hands shoulder high, hoping the woman understood they meant her no harm.

"We're not looking to cause any trouble, ma'am," Will said. He pointed at the badge pinned to his vest. "We're Texas Rangers, on our way to Del Rio. We were hoping we might be able to get a meal here, and bed down for the night. We've got a wounded boy with us who needs tending."

The woman narrowed her eyes to get a better look at them. Jamie had awakened. He moaned. The woman relaxed, just a trifle.

"I reckon y'all are who you say you are. Light and set a spell. Bring the boy right inside. I'm Maude Hawkins."

"Will Kirkpatrick, and my pardner, Jonas Peterson. The boy's Jamie. We never did get his last name."

"That don't matter none."

Maude called out three names.

"Josie, Harold. It's safe. Come out here and lend your ma a hand. Margaret Mary, I'll need you, too."

Will dismounted first. He ground tied Pete, then helped Jamie slide off Rebel. He had to drape Jamie's left arm over his shoulders to keep the boy from collapsing. Jonas dismounted, also ground tying his horse.

"Mercy sakes, that boy's hurt worse than you

let on," Maude exclaimed, seeing the bloody bandage wrapped around Jamie's middle. "What on earth happened to him?"

"He took a bullet in his back," Will answered. "I haven't been able to remove it. The slug's been in there too long. It needs to come out *pronto*."

"Bring him inside and lay him on the kitchen table. Margaret Mary, where are you?"

"I'm coming, Miz Maude," a lilting Irish voice from an unseen person inside answered. "I was out back, hanging clothes."

"Never mind you that. Get yourself into the kitchen. Clear off the table, and place a clean sheet on it. Then start water boiling. Gather plenty of towels and soap. The bottle of whiskey I keep for medicinal purpose. Hurry, child."

"I'll prepare those right away."

A young man of about twenty-four, along with a young woman of about twenty, appeared in the hallway. Both bore a strong resemblance to Maude, who was clearly their mother.

"Harold, help carry this boy into the kitchen and get him on the table. Josie, bring out the things we use for treating bullet wounds. Make it quick."

"Follow me," Maude ordered Will and Jonas. By now, one was on each side of Jamie, who was barely conscious, his arms hanging over their shoulders, his head lolling. His wound had begun to bleed again.

Jamie was taken into the kitchen, lifted onto the table, which was now covered by a clean white sheet, and helped to lie on his back.

"Jamie, can you hear me?"

"Yes . . . yes'm."

"Good. You're safe now, son. I'm Maude Hawkins. I'm going to get the bullet out of you. You'll stay here as long as it takes you to recover. Try and take it easy while I prepare to operate."

"You're . . . you're a doctor?"

"No, but I've treated plenty of bullet and knife wounds, not to mention broken bones, sprains, snake bites, and just plain sickness. I daresay I know more about caring for sick or hurt folks than most physicians."

"How might we help, ma'am?" Will asked.

"First, by not being impudent and 'ma'aming' me, young man. 'Ma'am' is for old ladies. My name's Maude. Second, by staying out from underfoot. I have three good helpers who all know what's required. Why don't you and your partner care for your horses, then clean up? There are plenty of empty stalls in the barn, plus hay and grain in the feed room. Toss some hay to the horses in the corral and check their water, if you don't mind. There's a pump and trough alongside the barn. You can water your horses, then wash up. You'll find washcloths, towels, and soap on a shelf in the feed room. The bunkhouse is empty, so you can pick any bunk you'd like. Plan on spending the night. We don't get much company here, and the kind we do get is usually the sort nobody wants. Now get out of the way so I can treat Jamie."

"Will, I think we'd better listen to the lady," Jonas said. "Let's go."

They retrieved their horses and led them inside the barn. After taking the gear off them and hanging the saddles, bridles, and saddle blankets on a stall door, they put their horses in adjoining stalls, filled their mangers with grain, then got them hay and filled their water buckets.

"Boy howdy, that Maude is certainly something else, Will. I'd let her side me in a gunfight any time."

"She's one tough cookie, all right," Will answered. "It also seems like she's solved our problem with where to leave Jamie. She's already hovering over him like an old mama hen with her only chick."

"I'm looking forward to a hot meal and a warm, clean bed for tonight. It still seems strange, though. The only ones here appear to be her, her son and daughter, and Margaret Mary, whoever she is."

"We'll have the chance to ask about that later. I just hope we get some straight answers. Meanwhile, let's finish caring for these horses and wash up ourselves."

Once they'd finished currying the horses,

leaving them munching on hay, Will and Jonas each took a washcloth, towel, and bar of Pears' soap from the feed room. They pulled off their hats, bandannas, vests and shrugged out of their shirts, hanging them on nails which served as clothes hooks. They also removed their shaving kits and a small mirror from their saddlebags.

"Boy howdy, cleaning up is gonna feel real good," Will said. "I think I'm carrying ten pounds of good Texas soil on my hide."

"I've got to be hauling around at least that much," Jonas answered.

They walked outside to the horse trough. First they ducked their heads into the water, soaking their hair, then straightening up, allowing the water to run over their shoulders and down their chests and backs. They ran the soap through their hair, working up a lather and scrubbing their scalps until they tingled. After ducking into the trough again to rinse the soap out of their hair, they washed their faces and upper torsos.

After washing, they scraped bits of soap into a shaving mug, added some water, and stirred it with a boar's hair shaving brush to work up a thick lather. They spread the soap over their faces and necks, then scraped away several days' growth of whiskers. Once that was done, they toweled off, then went back to the feed room and redressed.

"It's high time we checked on Jamie," Will said.

"He's gonna be all right," Jonas said. "He wouldn't dare die on that Hawkins woman. She'd bring him back to life just for spite, so she could kill him all over again if he did."

"I'd imagine that's so," Will agreed. He and Jonas broke into laughter.

After giving their horses each a leftover biscuit, they headed back to the house. A young woman of about eighteen greeted them. She had flaming red hair, emerald green eyes, a peaches and cream complexion with a smattering of freckles across her nose, and a nicely formed figure, with curves in all the right places and full, round breasts. She wore a white blouse and men's denims, which showed off that figure to full advantage. When she spoke, it was with a soft Irish brogue.

"Well, are ye gentlemen going to come inside, or do ye plan on standing there and givin' me the rovin' eyeballs all evening? Shure and begorrah, by me sainted mother, a body would swear ye'd never seen a woman before."

Will and Jonas blushed. Neither realized they had been staring at the lovely colleen.

"Beg, beg pardon, ma'am," Will stammered.

"Now listen to ye, callin' me 'ma'am.' If Miz Maude is too young to be 'ma'amed,' then I'm certainly not old enough. I'm Margaret Mary McGlynn. You may call me Margaret or Peggy. Either will do. Now follow me. And don't ye be trippin' over the rugs because you're watchin' me bum instead of where you're puttin' your big feet."

Margaret Mary led them to a back bedroom. Her walk was more of a sashay, her hips swaying inside those skin tight denims.

"The boy ye brought in is in there, along with Miz Maude. Ye can come on in, but don't be makin' too much noise. He's asleep, and needs to rest. Now I've got to scoot, before the ham burns. I'll see ye at supper."

"All right," Will said. "Thank you."

He and Jonas took off their hats and went into the room. Maude looked at them and put a finger to her lips.

Jamie was lying on the bed, covered with a sheet and light blanket. His skin was pale, but he was breathing regularly.

"How is he?" Will asked, speaking in a whisper.

"I was able to remove the bullet, clean, dress, stitch and bandage the wound," Maude answered. "Let's go to the parlor, where we can talk without waking him."

She led them into the front room, which held a large sofa and two overstuffed chairs. There was an oak table between the chairs, on which sat a large green glass ashtray. She waved them to the chairs, then took a seat on the sofa.

"You may smoke if you wish," she said. I'll be examining your injury after supper. Don't bother protesting. It will get you nowhere."

"I won't argue. Thank you, Maude," Will said. He and Jonas rolled and lit quirlies.

"How is Jamie?" Jonas asked.

"Right now he's sleeping comfortably. I would imagine he will sleep through the night, since he is quite weak, and exhausted. Obviously he's lost quite a large volume of blood. I was able to remove the bullet, cut away the dead flesh, clean the wound and stitch it shut. I loosely bandaged it, since the dressing will need to be changed when he wakes up. Would you please tell me his story, in particular how he ended up shot in the back, and with two Texas Rangers?"

"Not at all, although we don't know much about his background. We don't even know his last name," Will answered. "He says he's an orphan who lost his family to cholera."

"That's a terrible tragedy," Maude said. "I lost most of mine the same way, except it was dysentery that took my husband, my two oldest boys, and my three oldest girls."

"I'm so sorry for your loss," Will said.

"So am I," Jonas added. "I lost my family to sickness, too."

"How much do you know about the town of Sonora?" Will continued.

"Sonora? Just that it's a good place to stay away from."

"We found that out right quick," Will answered. "We stopped there for the night. A man named

Bob Adams, and his so-called wife, Suzanne, run the place."

"Make that ran the place," Jonas broke in.

"I'm getting to that. I'm trying to keep this short.

"Jamie warned us that the Adamses and some friends robbed and killed travelers who passed through Sonora and stopped for supplies, or spent the night. He learned they were suspicious of us, since we're Rangers. And planned to bushwhack us in our sleep. Sure enough, they did, had us way outnumbered, and pretty well cornered, even though thanks to Jamie's warning we were ready for them. Jamie had already done more than enough for us by slipping us extra ammunition, in addition to his warning. But he decided to do even more. He took a hand in the fight. Gunned down two of the outlaws. But one of them got him. Plugged him in the back, as you saw. Needless to say, we couldn't risk waiting to see if there were any more men coming for us, because we had no chance to fight them off. Naturally we had to take Jamie with us. We rode about fifteen miles south of town, until we found a good spot to hole up for the night. I did the best I could for Jamie, but couldn't get the bullet out. Two or three places we passed today offered food and water, but none would do anything about Jamie's wound. We're really obliged for all you've done."

"Why did the boy want to help you so badly?"

"After his family died, he had nowhere to live. It was his bad luck he wandered into Sonora. The Adamses made him a virtual slave. Suzanne Adams, or whatever her name really is, one time . . . I don't know if I should tell this to a lady."

"You don't have to. She forced the boy to have sex with her. He was desperate to get away from her."

"That's right. We're grateful to you and your family."

"*Por nada.* I only did what any decent person should. If you need any more assistance all you need do is ask."

"There's only one thing," Will said. "It's plain Jamie needs time to recuperate before he'll be able to travel. It's also obvious, even if we could wait until he's better, we can't take him along with us. We're hoping you'll take him in. We can pay for his care."

"Don't be ridiculous. Didn't you hear me say when you arrived the boy will remain here as long as necessary?"

"That's right kind of you," Will said.

"I'm doing it as much for me, and this ranch, as for Jamie. Y'all have had a chance to look around this place. It doesn't look like much now, but one time it was quite a spread. We raised short-horned beef cattle, which give much more meat and are less ornery than the old-fashioned longhorns. However, after my husband and five of my children passed, I lost all interest in maintaining the place. I've had plenty of offers to sell, but I just can't bring myself to do that. It also matters that Harold and Josie want to stay. So we've been doing just enough for the place to support ourselves."

"How does Jamie fit into all this?" Jonas asked.

"Over the past few months, I've come to the realization if Harold and Josie are to be able to hold onto this place after I'm gone, it needs to become a working ranch again. I've got enough capital to buy some good breeding stock and some decent cow ponies. What I will need is some hands to work the place. Once Jamie recovers, if he would be willing to stay here and learn how to handle cows and horses, he'd have a job for as long as he'd like. I might even end up adopting him, if things turn out that way. I can assure you he'd be well treated. Norris, my late husband, God rest his soul, treated everyone who worked for him fairly. He said that was the Lord's way, to share the bounty He'd given us with those who helped us succeed. That's how Margaret Mary came to us. She was working as a percentage girl at a saloon in Del Rio. Davey and Micah, my two oldest boys, were there having a few drinks when the owner started beating Margaret Mary for not wearing enough rouge and lipstick, not keeping the bodice of her dress pulled low enough, nor being friendly enough with the customers, in the Biblical meaning of friendly. They told him to stop, but instead of listening the man pulled a gun on them. That was the last thing he did this side of Hell. My boys shot him dead. Margaret Mary came to live with us. So you needn't worry about Jamie."

"That sounds like the best thing that could happen to the boy," Will said. "Otherwise he'd be right back where he was, homeless and hungry."

"Speaking of hungry, supper will be on the table in twenty minutes. That will give me just enough time to work on your wound now, Will, rather than afterwards."

Will and Jonas ate their fill of baked ham, boiled potatoes, homemade applesauce, pinto beans, hot-from-the-oven bread and freshly churned butter, and dried apple pie for dessert, all washed down with cups of strong black coffee. Now they were in the bunkhouse, settled on soft mattresses and ready to fall asleep.

"Boy howdy, Will, that little Irish gal sure is easy on the eyes," Jonas said. "I wouldn't mind getting to know her better. She's taken with me, too. Did you see the way she kept smiling at me? She couldn't keep her eyes off me all through supper. And she sure can cook, too. Best meal I've had in a month of Sundays."

"She was looking at me, not you, pal. Why settle for less than the best?"

"Dream on."

"It doesn't matter none who she was flirting with. Let me throw some cold water on your dreams. Harold intends for Margaret Mary to be his wife. She's willing, too. If you'd been paying any attention it's clear as day. If you'd tried to make a move on her, Harold would've gelded you like a rank stud colt. If you were lucky that would be all he did. Once he'd cut your balls off, he'd probably finish the job by slicing you open from your belly button to your throat."

"What about Josie then? She's a real pretty gal. And she's probably awfully lonesome living way out here with only her mother and her big brother. She might want to spend some time with me."

"Jonas, do you have a death wish? Would you really want to face Maude Hawkins and her shotgun if she found out you'd been messing with her daughter? It'd go worse for you than if Harold found you with Margaret Mary. She wouldn't just cut your balls off, she'd blow them clean into the next county. One barrel for each. That'd be a pretty ugly way to die. Also think of what your tombstone would say: 'Here lies Jonas Peterson, shot between the legs by an angry mother.' "

"I guess it wouldn't be worth the risk," Jonas conceded. "It's just that it's been way too long since I've been with a woman. Any kind of a woman."

"This from the *hombre* who used to be scared

to death of women. Boy howdy, you sure have changed. Listen, pardner. Tomorrow night we'll be in Del Rio. You'll have your pick of willing ladies to choose from. White, black, and plenty of Mexican *senoritas*. Just hold on until then. Now go to sleep. We've got to get an early start come morning. We've still got about forty-five miles to Del Rio."

13

Will and Jonas were fed a hearty breakfast before leaving for Del Rio. Jamie was still sleeping. Maude told the Rangers he had slept peacefully throughout the night, and his fever hadn't worsened. She would say good-bye for them when he awakened. Will told her they would stop by on their return trip from Del Rio, whenever that might be. What he left unsaid was he and Jonas would be coming by to make certain Jamie wasn't being mistreated. The boy had already suffered enough at the hands of Bob and Suzanne Adams.

They maintained a steady pace for the day, keeping the horses at either a jogtrot or mile-eating lope. They took several short stops to allow the mounts a rest, along with a longer one where they loosened Pete's and Rebel's cinches and took the bits from their mouths, allowing them to graze more comfortably while they themselves ate the ham sandwiches Margaret Mary had prepared for them.

A little less than nine hours after leaving the Hawkins' ranch, they reached Del Rio. With their early start, it was now just after two o'clock.

"The town's grown some," Will observed. "Quite a few new buildings."

"That looks like a brand-new hotel just ahead. It even appears to have its own livery stable," Jonas said, pointing to a freshly whitewashed adobe brick structure, four stories high. A sign hung out front. It was painted in florid red script, declared the place to be *La Casa Del Rio.* A smaller sign done in the same script hung beneath it. That one read *La Casa Del Rio Para Caballos.*

"You think we should give it a try?"

"I don't see why not," Will answered. "It's quite some time since I've been down this way. I recollect the hotel I stayed in during my last visit sure wasn't anything to write home about."

They rode up to the building, dismounted, looping their horses' reins over the hitch rail.

When they stepped into the lobby, Jonas let out a low whistle.

"Boy howdy, Will. This is the fanciest place I've ever been in. Can we even afford it?"

"The only way to know is to ask."

The *La Casa Del Rio*'s lobby was a light-filled, airy, spacious atrium, painted entirely in white, cream, and light yellow. It reached four stories to the building's roof, which was a skylight, a design depicting an intricate leaded glass motif of vibrantly colored flowers and tropical vines. Sunlight cascading through the stained glass lit up the lobby with constantly changing hues of every color imaginable as the sun moved across the sky, splashing the walls and floor in a remarkable display of brilliant color and light. The upper three floors were dedicated to rooms, which were set along open corridors around all four sides, which overlooked the lobby, adding to the sense of light and space. Two curved, intricately carved oak staircases led to those floors.

The center of the lobby was highlighted by a massive, three level cement fountain, the bowls of which were painted a sky blue, the columns decorated with mosaic tiles in a pale peach. The pool at the fountain's base held a number of colorful goldfish. The floor surrounding it was also mosaic, the rainbow colors of the glass chips glittering in the sun's rays, acting as prisms, scattering miniature rainbows throughout the entire first floor.

The lobby was furnished with deep red or green leather overstuffed couches and chairs, along with rattan side and coffee tables. Atop those tables were deep red, cut crystal lamps and ashtrays. Large palms in brightly patterned Mexican clay pots were strategically placed throughout the room.

At the rear of the lobby, as usual, was the reception desk. This one, however, was like none other either Will or Jonas had ever seen. It was gleaming white marble, which was streaked with dark red the color of partially dried blood. It was backed by pigeonholes carved from native Texas limestone.

Arranged along the left and right walls of the lobby were two restaurants, a saloon, a gentlemen's smoking lounge, alongside which was a tonsorial parlor with baths for men. There was also a salon with bathing facilities for ladies, and a small shop selling travel necessities and notions. In one corner stood a shoeshine stand. No bootblack or customer was there at the moment.

Will and Jonas walked past several people who were sitting in the lobby, some engrossed in conversation, others reading newspapers or letters. Most of them paid no attention to the new arrivals, only a few, their interest piqued by the silver star in silver circle badges pinned to the Rangers' vests, watched as they walked by.

The clerk on duty was a young woman, who appeared to be about the same age as Jonas. She stood close to five foot five inches tall and weighed around one hundred and fifteen pounds. She had hazel eyes, and her auburn hair was tied up in a bun at the nape of her neck. She was dressed in a starched white blouse with a high collar and puffed sleeves, along with a cotton floor length skirt, which was the same hue as the red in the marble. A red garnet hung from a gold chain around her neck. She filled out the outfit, which emphasized the curve of her hips and her nicely round, not overly large breasts, quite well. She all in all made a pleasing picture to the two trail weary lawmen.

She greeted them with a warm smile.

"Howdy, gents. Or I guess I should say Rangers. Welcome to the *La Casa Del Rio*. I'm Jennifer Coltraine. Are y'all interested in a room?"

"That depends," Will answered. "This place looks like it might be a little out of our reach. We weren't expecting anything this nice in little old Del Rio."

"It *is* the finest hotel in Del Rio. We've only been open for a few months. The *La Casa Del Rio* may be more affordable than you believe. Rooms run anywhere from one dollar to five dollars a night. The rate includes full breakfast in our *Rio Del Sol Dorado* restaurant. We serve dinner from eleven to two o'clock, and supper from five until nine in the evening, in our other restaurant, *El Jardin de la Bellezza y la Vida.* I assume you have horses."

"Yes, we do," Will answered.

"We have the best livery stable in Del Rio. The guest rate for boarding your animals is only fifty cents per night, per horse. That includes morning and evening grain, all the hay they require, and water. Grooming also, of course. We have a hostler on duty twenty-four hours, seven days a week. The hotel also employs a full-time farrier, should your horses' hooves need attention. If you decide not to stay with us, but still wish to board your horses in our stable, the boarding rate doubles to one dollar per day, and grooming is an extra twenty-five cents for each rubdown. So the question, gentlemen, is not whether you *can* afford to stay at the *La Casa Del Rio*, but rather whether you can afford not to?"

"Jennifer, you make a mighty convincing argument," Will said. "What are the rates for the two of us?"

"Not to mention you're awful pretty," Jonas added.

Jennifer blushed.

"Why, thank you. But back to business. How long would you be staying? What type of room would you require?"

"Let's say two weeks to start," Will answered. "We might not be here every night, but we would like to keep the room available."

"One bed or two?"

"Two," Jonas said, before Will had the chance to reply.

"We have several available. The second floor will be one dollar per night. Third is either one dollar or two dollars per night. The more expensive rooms overlook the *Rio Grande*. Fourth floor is either three or four dollars per night. The three-dollar rooms provide a city view, the four-dollar rooms overlook the river. There are two five-dollar rooms, our best. They are corner suites which overlook both the city and river. The weekly rate for either of those is thirty dollars, which would save you ten dollars for the two week stay. You would also receive a reduced rate for boarding your horses of two dollars and fifty cents for the week, per animal."

"We'll take the one facing north and west," Will answered, without hesitation. Jonas looked at him with incredulity.

"Excellent. It is already made up and ready for you to occupy. We do require payment in full, in advance. However, you will be allowed to charge any meals you order in the hotel, any personal services such as haircuts, shaves, baths, or shining your boots to your rooms. We also offer take-out laundry service for your convenience. Those charges are due at the end of each week."

She gave Will and Jonas a wan smile, her gaze lingering on the old bullet scar along Will's right cheekbone. The wound had occurred several years previously, but still stood out starkly against his deeply bronzed skin.

Will pulled out his billfold and removed two hundred-dollar yellowback bank notes, issued by the Kirkpatrick State Bank, his family's.

"Here you are, Jennifer. Keep five dollars for yourself, and hold the rest for any charges which accrue to our account."

"Why thank you very much, Ranger Kirkpatrick. Now if you would kindly sign the register, I'll prepare your receipt, give you the keys to your room, and a stable ticket for your horses."

While Will signed his and Jonas's names on the register, Jennifer pulled two sets of keys from one of the top pigeonholes. She handed those to Will, along with a cardstock ticket for the stable, which had columns to keep track of its charges.

"Room 410," she said. "I'm certain you'll enjoy your stay with us. There is a sheet of paper in the room listing all of our services, and the hours our restaurants and shops are open. I'll be going off duty at five, but if you don't come down before then, we're certain to see each other before you leave."

"Thank you," Will said. "C'mon, Jonas, let's get the horses settled and some rest for ourselves."

Jonas didn't seem to hear him.

"I said, *c'mon,* Jonas."

Jonas blushed.

"Oh. Sorry, Will. I guess my mind was elsewhere."

"I guess it was," Will retorted.

Jonas had been staring at the pretty young desk clerk.

After leaving their horses in the capable charge of a young Mexican hostler, the two Rangers, their saddlebags slung over their shoulders and toting their Winchesters, climbed the stairs to their fourth-floor room. Both were slightly winded when they reached the top. They went to the room, Will fumbling with the key until he managed to insert it in the lock and open the door.

Jonas walked in ahead of his partner, tossed his saddlebags on a luggage stand, and looked around in disbelief.

"Boy howdy, Will, this place is sure something," he exclaimed. "Just look at the furniture. Those beds appear as if a man could sink into 'em and never come up again. You can see clear into old *Ciudad Acuna* from the windows."

Unlike most frontier hostelries, the *La Casa Del Rio* was sumptuously furnished. The furniture was French Empire, intricately carved pieces of oak and walnut. The beds were both doubles, with thick mattresses, covered with satin sheets and feather ticks. The floor was parquet, the wood polished to a high shine. Thick woolen throw rugs were at the foot of each bed. There were two leather and oak armchairs, two bedside tables, and a writing desk, on which sat an inkwell, quill pens, a blotter, and stationery. The lamps on each table and the desk were amber glass and cut crystal, topped by a globe shade painted with yellow roses and blue forget-me-nots, from which dangled crystal pendants. Lace doilies were under each lamp. Paintings of various flowers in vibrant hues hung on the wall above each bed. In the style of the times, the walls were papered in a cabbage rose pattern.

The windows were open to catch the breeze off

the river. Sheer curtains fluttered across them, while heavy blue velvet drapes were tied back to the sides.

There were not one, but two individual washstands, each backed with gilt framed mirrors. A pitcher filled with water, basin, soap, shaving mugs, ladies' hand mirrors, sandalwood combs, and ivory hair brushes, stacks of washcloths and towels, were on each. Towel rods were attached to both sides of the stands.

"I wonder what's in here," Will said.

He opened the door to what he assumed was a closet.

"Look here, pardner. It's a separate room for the commodes. We won't have to go all the way downstairs to use the privy. There's a sign which says the maid will clean in here daily, so we won't even have to clean up after ourselves."

The room held two commodes with chamber pots and lids. There was a small table in between, which held stacks of neatly cut paper for cleaning when done, a small pitcher, basin, and soap. There was even a small, high up window, open at the top and bottom, to let in fresh air and remove any lingering foul odors.

Jonas poked his head inside the room.

"Well I'll be damned. What'll they think of next?"

"I've heard tell some places in the big cities, especially like New York or Philadelphia back east, have real bathtubs and commodes with running water in every room. Some even have hot water."

"You're joshin' me, Will."

"On my honor as a Texas Ranger and a Kirkpatrick, I am not. My father's even talked about getting one for our house."

"Knowing your father, it'll happen, if it hasn't already," Jonas said. "Get outta my way, pard. I'm gonna make good use of this here facility, and I mean right now!"

Jonas shoved Will aside, went into the room, and slammed the door shut.

"How long are you gonna be in there?" Will shouted after him.

"I dunno, but don't hold your breath. On second thought, mebbe you *should* hold it."

"The hell with it. I'm just gonna take a nap," Will answered.

He pulled off his boots, hat, bandanna and gun belt, then stretched out on the bed nearest the door.

Half an hour later, Jonas emerged.

"You asleep, Will?"

"I was just about."

"You need to use the commode?"

"Nah. I reckon that can wait until after I catch some sleep."

"Grabbing some shut-eye does sound like a fine idea."

Jonas also partially undressed and got into the other bed. He lay on his back, looking at the embossed tin ceiling.

"You thinking about anything in particular, Will?"

"Just getting some sleep that it seems you're determined I'm not going to have. Why don't you just turn over, shut up, and let me get some?"

"Do you mind if I ask you a couple of questions?"

"Will it make any difference whether I do or not?"

"I guess it won't."

"Then go ahead. Ask 'em."

"All right. What did you think of that Jennifer gal? She sure is a looker."

"That's all you're worried about?"

"No. I was just wondering if you noticed her lookin' at me? She sure seemed taken with my good looks."

"Hah. You, Jonas? Good looks! She was staring at me, not you."

"The only thing about you she was staring at is that bullet scar you're carrying on your cheek, pard. It's plain as the nose on your face it's me she's interested in."

"Keep on dreaming. This scar makes me look more rugged. Women can't resist it. Is that all you wanted to bother me about? If you need to be with a woman that bad, I'm sure we won't have any problem finding you a willing one. Me neither, for that matter."

"No, that's not all. I'm curious as to why you chose a room clear up on this floor. Yeah, it's nice, best one I've ever been in, but it's damned expensive."

"There's only two reasons. One, from up here, we have a clear view of the river. We can see anyone coming across from Mexico, including those who might be bent on causin' trouble. We can also spot anyone coming into town from the north and west. Two, if a fight starts while we're in this room, we have the advantage of bein' up high. Gives us a better shot. Does that answer your question?"

"It does. I also like being above the dust and noise from the street. And being up this high makes it harder for anyone with the idea to ambush us. How long do you plan on staying here? I know what you told the clerk, but I'm damn sure we won't be here for an entire two weeks."

"We won't be. I plan on staying in town for a couple of days, asking questions. We'll check in with the local law tomorrow. With any luck we'll get a few leads on this *El Atrevido hombre*. Whether or not we do, after we've found out what we can, we'll head for Coffee City. I want to make one thing plain, pardner. We're not goin' back to Sweetwater until we run him and his entire outfit to ground. We're not givin' up until he and his men are behind bars or dead. Or we are."

"Us behind bars?" Jonas said, chuckling. "It seems to me I could've been there already, without goin' through all this trouble."

"You know what I mean. The only way *El Atrevido* will escape is if he leaves us both lying dead in the dirt. Now if you're done asking foolish questions let me get to sleep. We'll go for supper in a couple of hours."

14

Shortly after six, Will and Jonas started down to the hotel's main restaurant. Jonas was disappointed to learn Jennifer had already gone home, despite the fact she had told him and Will her shift ended at five.

Will gave Jonas a slap on the back.

"Don't worry about that gal for tonight, pardner. After we have our supper and a few drinks, we'll ask around as to where we might find some feminine entertainment. Besides, she must already have a steady beau, pretty as she is. You can bet your hat she's not looking for a fiddle-footed Texas Ranger who can't ever stay in one place for long. If you keep this up, one of these days you'll get yourself shot dead by a jealous husband or boyfriend. And I won't be there to stop him."

Jonas laughed.

"I would hope you wouldn't. That would be mighty strange. Right now the only thing I'm worried about is filling my belly with some decent chuck."

"That makes two of us."

Will laughed to himself as they descended the stairs.

Boy howdy, how Jonas has changed. The first

time I took him to visit some soiled doves, he was petrified. It turned out he'd never been with a woman before. Once he got through that night, everything was different. Now I can't hardly stop him from searching out the first brothel he can find, every new town we come to.

They had just started to cross the lobby when the thundering hooves of galloping horses, accompanied by heavy gunfire, reverberated through the hotel.

"Trouble!" Jonas exclaimed.

He and Will reversed direction, pulled out their revolvers, and raced outside. Pandemonium greeted them. Masked gunmen were running their horses up and down the street, shooting at anyone who moved. Their attack seemed concentrated on the Val Verde County Sheriff's Office. Bullets shattered its windows and splintered its front door.

"This way, Jonas!"

Running low, zigzagging, the Rangers ran toward the building, firing on the way. Jonas hit one of the raiders in the back, knocking him from his horse. Jonas slid behind a horse trough, pushed the empties from his Smith and Wesson, then reloaded. Bullets punching through the wooden sides of the trough sent miniature geysers into the air, splattering him.

Will had taken cover behind the scant protection of a porch roof support post. He shot one raider off his horse, shot another in the shoulder, sending him riding out of the fray, then had to dive to his belly when some of the raiders concentrated their fire on his position. Two more went down, shot by whom Will knew not. Nor would he ever find out. He rose to one knee, aimed carefully, and put a bullet through another man's gut. The man screamed, slumped over his horse's neck, then slid to the road.

Jonas had reloaded his Smith and Wesson yet again. He emptied the .44's chamber into a tightly bunched group of men, every bullet finding a target.

Suddenly aware they were facing more opposition than they'd expected, their numbers cut at least by half, the remaining raiders wheeled their horses around and galloped out of Del Rio, chased by the bullets being sent their way. One took a bullet in his back. He fell from the saddle, his right foot caught in the stirrup. His panicked horse dragged him after the rest of the fleeing gang.

"You all right, Jonas?" Will called.

"Yeah. You?"

"I'm fine. Nary a scratch," Will answered. "Let's see if any of these *hombres* are still alive and able to talk. I sure hope so."

A man carrying a doctor's bag, who had spotted Will's badge, came up.

"Ranger! Doctor Patterson. Where might I be of most help?"

"Head for the sheriff's office. The sons of bitches poured a lot of lead into it. Thanks, Doc."

The physician waved acknowledgment at Will as he turned toward the office.

With the gunfire stopped and the raiders run off, people were starting to emerge from hiding, beginning to offer aid and comfort to the injured. An unknown number of townspeople had been wounded or killed.

Seven of the raiders lay in the street, four of them dead, two gravely wounded, and one with a serious but non-life-threatening shoulder wound. There was no way of knowing how many of the raiders who'd fled had been shot, nor how badly.

Will hunkered alongside the most grievously wounded man, who'd taken a bullet in the middle of his belly. Blood quickly spreading across his shirtfront indicated at least one major blood vessel had been severed. He would bleed out in a matter of minutes.

"*Hombre*, you don't have long. You might want to make peace with your Maker before it's too late. It'd help if you told me who you work for, and why Del Rio was targeted."

The man fixed his gaze on Will's badge.

"Bastard. You can . . . go to Hell . . . Ranger. I ain't gonna . . . talk."

"You certain?"

"Damn straight. I'm certain."

Will nodded at Jonas.

"I'm about to change your mind," Jonas said.

He put his right foot down on the man's middle, his bootheel directly over the bullet hole in his gut, and started pressing.

"Gonna talk yet?"

The man shook his head.

"Well then."

Jonas lifted his foot about six inches, brought it down hard on the man's belly, then drove his bootheel as deeply into the gut as he could.

The dying outlaw screamed, writhing in a vain attempt to escape the pain of Jonas's boot sunk deep into his bullet torn gut.

"El Atrevido! He has vowed vengeance . . . he will never . . . be defeated. Never . . . Never . . . Nev . . ."

Jonas removed his foot from the now dead man's belly.

"I told you you'd talk, you son of a bitch."

"We've got a start," Will said. "Let's see if the others will give us anything."

The second of the three wounded men had also breathed his last. This left the man with the shoulder wound. He was lying face down.

When Will rolled him over, he shoved the knife he'd kept hidden under his body into his stomach, before he could be stopped.

"*Viva El Atrevido*!"

Those were his final words.

"He's not gonna talk, Will."

"Tell me something I don't already know."

A group of men approached.

"Ranger, is there anything we can do?" one asked.

"Yeah," Will answered. "Take these dead *hombres* and drag them outta the street. Then meet me and my pardner at the sheriff's office. We'll figure out our next steps from there."

"Right away. You heard the man. Let's get to work."

Will and Jonas hurried into the sheriff's office. Three deputies were sprawled dead on the floor. Doctor Patterson was working on a fourth man, whom he had lifted onto a desk. The man's shirt was open, revealing a bullet hole in his right breast.

Patterson glanced at the Rangers when they walked in.

"If you wish to speak with the sheriff, you'd better do it now. I'm about to probe for the bullet in his chest. I'm not certain whether or not I'll be able to save his life."

"*Gracias*, Doc," Will said.

He stood next to the wounded sheriff, whose eyes were glassy and breathing labored. Pink froth bubbling from his mouth and nose indicated the bullet had punctured a lung. Such a wound was almost invariably a death sentence.

"Sheriff, can you hear me? I'm Texas Ranger Will Kirkpatrick."

"John La Patrie. Didn't know . . . Rangers . . . were in town."

"Me and my pardner just pulled in earlier. We were gonna stop by and see you and the marshal first thing in the morning. I'm guessing you already know who's behind this raid."

"*El . . . Atrevido.*"

"Do you happen to know his reason?"

"I made . . . a deal with . . . the Devil. Knew me . . . and my deputies . . . could never handle his gang. Too many men . . . too easy for them to escape . . . into Mexico. You . . . Rangers won't, either . . . unless you brought . . . an entire troop."

"It's just the two of us."

"Then take my advice. Turn and run, or wind up . . . dead."

Will shook his head.

"No can do, Sheriff. You know that. What do you mean, you made a deal with the Devil?"

La Patrie seemed to have a brief burst of strength.

"I told the son of a bitch if he stayed out of Val Verde County I wouldn't bother him. That changed when . . . he moved into Coffee City. Went and . . . palavered with him. Told him if he didn't . . . move on I'd send for . . . the Rangers. Big mistake. Should have just gut shot the bastard . . . when I had . . . the chance. Had a good thing goin' . . . with him. When he raided ranches or committed robberies . . . just inside the county line . . . we'd split the money. Worked . . . for quite a spell. Then he got greedy, and I grew a conscience. Worst thing that can . . . happen to a man . . . lettin' guilt . . . eat away at him."

Patterson broke in.

"Ranger, you've got to end this conversation if I'm to have any chance of saving this man."

"Just one last question, Doc."

"Make it short."

"Sheriff, who is *El Atrevido*?"

"Someone you'd . . . never suspect."

"Give me a name."

"Can't . . . just . . . can't."

La Patrie's eyes closed.

"He's unconscious, Ranger. It will be a miracle if he lasts the rest of the night," Patterson said.

"Try your best to keep him alive," Will answered. "Me and my pardner are staying at the *La Casa Del Rio*. You can get word to us there. Now to see what kind of shape the rest of this town is in."

It was close to three in the morning before Will and Jonas were able to return to their room. Since it would be futile to attempt to follow *El Atrevido*'s men in the dark, and with the odds of their being ambushed too great to ignore, they chose to take to the trail at first light, snatching a bit of sleep in the meantime.

Before turning in they located Del Rio City

Marshal Sandy Becker and his two deputies. The Marshal's Office had not been targeted in the raid. The local lawmen did take part in the defense of the town, helping to drive off the surviving gang members. One of the deputies had taken a bullet through his left thigh for his trouble. Will appointed Becker and his deputies Special Texas Rangers, which gave them authority as lawmen for all of Val Verde County. They would replace Sheriff La Patrie, who even if he survived would be placed under arrest, and the deceased county deputies. All three appeared to be honest, upstanding lawmen. The Rangers and the local lawmen were soon on a first name basis.

They also located Del Rio's Mayor, Horatio Adcock. He had little information to add. He agreed to meet with Will and Jonas the next day, after they returned from attempting to follow the trail of the raiders.

Once certain there were no other raiders hiding in town, no one else to be questioned, the dead removed and the injured treated, they were finally able to call it a night.

"You know, Will," Jonas said, as he flopped face down on his bed, "we never did get that chuck. Or any women. Damn that *El Atrevido*."

Their search the next morning lasted just a short time. As both men had expected, the tracks of the gang's horses only remained on the Texas side of the Rio Grande for less than two miles, before they went into the muddy waters of the river.

"This is as far as we go for now," Will said.

"What do you want to do next?" Jonas asked. "Ride on up to Coffee City and see what we can scare up?"

"Not for two or three days. I want to do some more pokin' around in Del Rio first. We'll go through the sheriff's records, and any of his personal papers. There might be a good lead somewhere in them. See if anyone we talk with can give us any little scrap of information that might be helpful. Talk with the bartenders, barbers, storekeepers and the whores. They hear things most others don't."

"You're not worried *El Atrevido* might slip back into Mexico?"

"After what happened last night, if he's gonna do that he already has, which means it's too late for us to catch up with him. However, I've got a gut feeling he's gonna stay right where he's at. That raid was a challenge. He's daring anyone to try and take him. If he hadn't already been aware we were in Del Rio, after last night he damn sure is. He'll expect us to come charging into Coffee City before sundown tonight. We're gonna fool him. Stay in Del Rio for a bit, let him think we've got something planned he doesn't know about. Rumors, time, and waiting can make even the most confident man nervous. And nervous men make mistakes."

"So do nervous lawmen," Jonas pointed out.

"But that ain't us. Is it?"

"Nope, not us."

15

Will and Jonas spent the next two days talking to everyone they could in Del Rio, attempting to ascertain if anyone had the least idea of *El Atrevido*'s true identity. They stopped and had drinks at every saloon in the city, visited most of the stores and businesses, ate at several restaurants. They got shaves, haircuts, and baths at their hotel's tonsorial parlor. They spoke to the hostlers at all three livery stables in the city. Visited the houses of ill repute, the gambling parlors and dance halls. No one could, or would, admit to knowing anything about *El Atrevido* or any member of his gang.

"Tomorrow we leave for Coffee City," a frustrated Will told Jonas as they were returning to their hotel. "You can be positive if we don't find *El Atrevido* or someone who can take us to him, he'll be certain to come after us."

"That sounds good to me," Jonas agreed. "I'm tired of wastin' time and getting nowhere."

When they walked into the hotel's lobby, movement and a flash of light reflecting off something metallic from the dimly lit back wall of the fourth-floor balcony caught their attention. They each dove to the side as gunfire crackled. Two bullets smacked into the floor behind them.

They pulled out their pistols and fired at the riflemen readying to take second shots. Both hit their target. One of the men clutched his chest, fell back, and slumped to the floor. The other yelled, grabbed at his stomach, then folded, catching the railing at his waist. He somersaulted over the railing, his scream of terror cut short when he landed head first on the lobby floor, snapping his neck, his skull bursting open like an overripe cantaloupe. The few people in the lobby screamed and scattered for cover. Jennifer, who was covering the evening shift for a sick colleague, crawled under the reception desk.

Powder smoke hung in the air, but no more shots came.

Will pointed to one man.

"You. Go find the marshal or one of his deputies."

"Yessir, Ranger."

"Jonas, check the *hombre* upstairs. I'll look at the one who fell."

Jonas took the stairs two at a time. Will went to look at the would-be ambusher who had plunged from the balcony.

Will's man was obviously dead.

"Is your man still alive?" he yelled up to Jonas.

"Nope."

"Better drag him downstairs."

"Too much damn work, Will."

Jonas picked up the dead man and flung him

off of the balcony. The body hit the floor a few feet away from his dead partner.

"Comin' right down."

Jonas rushed to rejoin Will. Neither of them recognized the dead men.

"Jennifer!" Jonas called. "Jennifer!"

No answer.

"I'll get her," Jonas said.

He went over to the desk, leaned under it and spoke softly. In a few minutes, Jennifer came out. With Jonas's arm around her shoulder, she walked over to Will.

"Jennifer, I'm sorry, but I have to ask if you recognize either of these men," Will said.

Shaking, she looked at both their faces.

"No. No, I don't."

"You've never seen them before?"

Jennifer shook her head. "No. Do you mind if I go now? I need to get out of here."

"All right. Thank you. You can leave. Will your boss allow that?"

"I might lose my job, but I can't be alone here."

"Jennifer, I can spend the rest of the night down here until your relief person arrives. That way you'd have someone with you," Jonas offered. "Would that help?"

"It would make me feel better. I'm so terribly frightened."

"That's understandable. Will, would my staying with Jennifer until her relief arrives be all right?"

"It's fine with me. She'll have to wait until we finish up our work here, though. And where's the damn marshal? Excuse my language, Jennifer."

"I'll stay with her while you work, Ranger," a matronly woman offered. "My name is Monica Xander. She'll be fine with me."

"We appreciate that, ma'am," Will answered. "But what in the blue blazes is taking the marshal so long?"

"I'm right here, Will," Marshal Becker said, as he walked through the door. "What the devil's it all about this time?"

Will nodded at the bodies.

"These two jaspers tried to ambush us. It's lucky some light reflected off one of their rifle barrels, or they would have succeeded. That gave us just enough time to get out of the way of the bullets they sent after us. We were able to drill them before they got off another shot."

Becker looked at the dead men.

"I know these two. Henry Knowlton and Pete Savage. They work at the Circle H Ranch. It's a little more than halfway between here and Coffee City."

"Well, I'd say they don't work there no more," Jonas drawled.

"I guess 'worked there' *would* be more accurate," Becker conceded.

"Sandy, who owns the Circle H?"

"Some Eastern syndicate. The manager's an

hombre name of Duke McDougal. I've met him a few times. He seems like a straight shooter."

"Do you think the syndicate might be backing *El Atrevido*? They could be using him as a way to gain control of more land."

"I suppose it's possible, but my gut says no. There's been no evidence of them running wet cattle. They've also been hit a few times by rustlers. I'm thinking if these two were workin' for *El Atrevido*, they were freelancing. Maybe they were hired just to kill you two."

"Me'n Jonas will be stopping by the place on our way to Coffee City. We'll notify McDougal about what happened, and let him know to see you, to have the bodies released to him. Where exactly is the place?"

"There's a little settlement called Comstock about thirty miles from here. The Circle H is two miles before that. The main gate's right on the road to Coffee City. You can't miss it."

"*Bueno*. We're obliged. Sandy, there's not a helluva lot more me'n Jonas can do here. Would you mind finishing up? I don't know how long we'll be in Coffee City. Write up your report as soon as you get the chance. I'll put it with mine when we return, and send them both off to Austin."

"Sure. That won't be a problem, except for one thing."

"What's that?"

“The odds are neither of you will come back. Not only will y’all be up against *El Atrevido* and his men, most of the population won’t help. That son of a bitch is some kind of hero to them. At best they just won’t cooperate with you. At worst they’ll try’n stick a knife in your back.”

“Then we’ll just have to make certain that doesn’t happen, won’t we?”

“Might be easier said than done.”

“We’ll see. Jonas, you comin’ along?”

“I’ll be with you once Jennifer’s relief takes over. Don’t wait up.”

“I don’t plan to. Sandy, we’ll check in with you before we leave town.”

“I’d appreciate that, Will. Get some sleep. You’ll need it.”

16

Jennifer's relief arrived just before eleven.

"Jennifer, I heard about the shooting. Are you all right?"

"I am now. Jonas, this is Jack Goulding. Jack, Texas Ranger Jonas Peterson."

The two men shook hands.

"I'm pleased to meet you, Ranger."

"The same here."

Goulding was in his fifties, a little shorter than average, slightly pudgy, mostly bald but with a fringe of gray hair. He had a ready smile and a firm grip. He walked with a limp. Both men immediately liked each other.

"Jennifer, you need to go home and get some rest," Goulding said.

"I plan on doing just that. Jonas, I know you have to get up early to leave for Coffee City, but would you be a dear and walk me home? I'm still terribly frightened. I don't live far from here."

"Of course," Jonas agreed. "Lead the way. Nice meeting you, Jack. We'll probably run across each other again."

"I'm certain we will. Jennifer, before you leave, is there anything I should know about?"

"Nothing I know of. Oh, that nice Mrs. Xander in Room 307 helped me a lot during the whole awful shooting. I promised her a free session in the ladies' salon."

"It will be arranged," Goulding promised. "Good night, Jennifer, Ranger."

"Good night, Jack."

"G'night," Jonas added.

Jennifer's house was a small whitewashed adobe cottage, about a five-minute walk from the hotel. She clung more tightly to Jonas as they drew near.

"Jennifer, are you sure you'll be all right?"

"I . . . I'm not certain. What if there's someone inside? I thought the *Casa Del Rio* was one of the safest places in the city, and look what happened there."

She shivered.

"Would I be asking too much to have you come in with me, just in case?"

"Of course not. I'll be happy to."

"*Muchas gracias*. You are a true gentleman."

"I wouldn't go that far."

The adobe consisted of three small rooms, a living room, kitchen/dining area, and a bedroom. The first two were empty.

The bedroom was also unoccupied. When Jonas turned to leave it, Jennifer was standing in the doorway, blocking his path. She was unbuttoning her white blouse, revealing her cleavage and much of her nicely rounded breasts.

"Jonas, do you really have to leave right now?"

Jonas swallowed hard. He felt warm, his heart pounding and blood racing.

"I guess I could stay a while. Just to make sure you're safe."

"Of course. Just to make sure I am safe."

Jennifer nudged Jonas toward the bed. She lifted her lips to his, and kissed him. Her right hand slid inside his shirt and began massaging his chest. The left undid the shirt buttons. She slid it off his shoulders. Her hands drifted lower. The kisses became more passionate.

Something heavy clubbed Jonas on the back of his neck, right at the base of his skull. The room swirled, then went black.

17

Will awoke when the first rays of the sun streaked through the window. He lay still for a moment, yawned, stretched, then scratched his belly. He looked over at Jonas's bed and cursed.

"Dammit. Where is that woman *loco* son of a bitch? He knows we're supposed to be leaving first thing. I should have realized when he stayed with that gal he'd end up in bed with her. Now I've gotta track him down."

Will hurriedly dressed and went downstairs. Jack Goulding was still behind the front desk.

"May I help you, Ranger?"

"I hope so. My pardner was down here last night. He never came up to our room. Do you happen to know where he went?"

"I do. Jennifer was still frightened. She asked your partner to accompany her home. Are you saying he never came back? I apologize I didn't notice, but I have to admit I dozed off."

"That's what it appears. Do you know where Jennifer lives?"

"It's about a ten-minute walk. Just beyond the haberdashery there's a row of small adobes. Hers is the last one. It's whitewashed, unlike the others. You can't miss it."

"I'm obliged."

"I hope you find him soon, Ranger," Goulding called after Will.

Will shouted back over his shoulder.

"He'll be sorry when I do."

Getting his horse saddled and bridled would have taken more time than walking, so Will hoofed it over to Jennifer's house. Not worried about waking anyone, nor catching them in a compromising position, he pounded on the door, then slammed it open. A scream came from the bedroom. Will rushed there.

Jennifer was in bed. No one else was with her. She had pulled the sheets up to her chin.

"Ranger! How dare you break into my house. What do you want?"

"I'm lookin' for my pardner. The desk clerk says he brought you home. Where the hell is he?"

"Your language! I'm a lady. You shouldn't speak that way in front of a lady."

"Never mind my damn language. Where's Jonas?"

"I have no idea. He accompanied me home, then went on his way. He never even came in the house. I invited him in, but he was too much of a gentleman to accept."

"I highly doubt that. I know him a helluva lot better than you do. I'm going to look around. Do you have any objections?"

"Would it matter if I did?"

"No, it would not."

"Then look away. You won't find anything."

"I'll let you know."

Jennifer stayed in bed while Will examined the house. He went through it with a fine-toothed comb, then examined the ground outside. A patch of disturbed soil directly under the bedroom window, showing rust-colored patches, caught his attention. He stooped to study it more closely.

Will picked up some of the soil and let it fall through his fingers. He looked at a jumble of footprints, drag marks, then the hoofprints of three horses, heading from behind the house toward the northwest. He shook his head.

"Damn, Jonas. What the hell did you get yourself into, partner?"

He went back inside. Jennifer had gotten out of bed. She was covered with a light pink cotton wrapper.

"Well, did you find anything?"

"I thought you said Jonas didn't come in your house."

"He didn't."

"You're lying. There's blood spatters on your floor. You see that curtain rod over your window?"

"Yeah. What about it?"

"There were drapes hanging from it. You can see some threads. I'm guessing someone was hiding behind those. Jonas must've gotten careless and didn't pay attention. Probably because the only thing he was interested in was you. I'd guess you kept him busy until someone bashed him over the head. Then he was dragged out through the window. Either the drapes were pulled down by mistake or because Jonas's blood was on them. There's scuff marks on the sill. He was hauled off on horseback. Am I close?"

"I have no idea what you're talking about. Jonas walked me home because I was scared and asked him to. Then he left."

"I'm gonna find him. And when I do, you'd damn well better hope he's alive. Because if he's not, there ain't anywhere in the entire State of Texas you'll be able to hide from me. Nor for the people you're working with. That's a promise."

Will slammed the door behind him as he left. He hurried back to the hotel, answered Goulding's brief question with a no, he hadn't found Jonas, then went to his room, gathered both his and Jonas's gear, and went to the hotel's stable. As he'd suspected, Jonas's horse was still in his stall, as was Pete. The hostler on duty came in from one of the corrals.

"*Buenos dias*, Ranger Will."

"*Buenos dias*, Pablo. Have you seen my partner?"

"Ranger Jonas? No, I have not. You are the first person to come by since *ultima noche*."

"Get Ranger Jonas's *caballo* ready, while I saddle up Pete."

"Has something happened to him?"

"I don't know for certain yet, Pablo. I've got to look for him. When I find him, and I will, he'll need his *caballo*."

What Will left unsaid was that he might well need Jonas's horse to bring back his body.

"*Si*, *lo entiendo*. I will prepare his *caballo* for the journey."

"Take these."

Will handed Pablo Jonas's rifle and saddlebags.

"Of course, Ranger."

The horses were ready in less than five minutes. Will climbed into his saddle. Pablo handed him Rebel's lead rope.

"*Buena suerte y que Dios te acompane*."

"*Gracias*, Pablo. *Por favor*, let Marshal Becker know what has happened."

"I will do that."

Will fought the urge to put Pete into an immediate gallop. Crippling his horse by not warming him up first would help no one, least of all Jonas. He kept Pete at a walk until they reached the edge of town, then put him into a mile eating lope.

18

Once he was on the main road, Will had no way of picking out the hoofprints belonging to the horses of the men he was following from all the others. He was going by his hunch that Jonas was still alive, and been taken to Coffee City. He uttered a silent prayer that he was right.

Will's first stop was at the Circle H Ranch. A wrangler took him to Duke McDougal, the ranch's manager. McDougal greeted him with a broad smile, almost as wide as his bushy moustache, and hearty handshake.

"Howdy, Ranger. I understand you wanted to see me. Care for some coffee?"

"I don't have much time."

"It's already boiled. Cookie, bring us two cups of coffee."

"Right away, Boss."

The grizzled old cowboy who was now the ranch cook shuffled off.

"Now, Ranger, what's the reason you're here?"

"Two of your men. Henry Knowlton and Pete Savage. They tried to ambush me and my pardner last night. They're both dead."

The normally affable McDougal grew somber.

"Both of them? I'm not surprised. You should know I fired them a little over a month ago. They didn't get along with the other hands. I was also suspicious they might have been in cahoots with the rustlers who have been raiding this ranch. Ah, here comes Cookie with our coffee."

McDougal waited until the cook was back inside before continuing the conversation.

"Do you know why they attempted to kill you? I suspect it's not just because you're a lawman."

"No, it's not. Jonas, my pard, and I were sent down here to capture *El Atrevido* and break up his gang. I believe Knowlton and Savage were hired by *El Atrevido* to get rid of us."

"Permanently."

"Yeah. Permanently."

"What happened to your partner?"

"I know he was led into a trap. It appears he was caught settin', distracted by a young woman. The signs indicate he was still alive, and kidnapped. The few tracks I could follow headed in this direction. I figure he's bein' taken to Coffee City."

"The Daring One's headquarters. That makes sense. You'll probably be promised your pard will be returned to you safely if you quit the chase and leave the territory."

"We both know such a promise ain't worth a plugged wooden nickel."

"So you're headed straight into the cougar's den."

"That's right."

"You want some help? I can spare half a dozen men. There's no one or nowhere safe around here until *El Atrevido* is gone."

"I might take you up on that, after I get a better handle on the situation. Too many men right now might scare that son of a bitch off. For certain if he's got Jonas he'd have him killed. I have to go in alone, see what I'm up against."

"I understand. But I also understand you'll never root out that bastard without help. Not even though you're a Ranger. I've got an idea."

"I'm willing to listen."

"Coffee City's the nearest town, so it's where the ranch gets its supplies. It's about time for another run. I can send someone anytime now. Why don't I give you say, four days to ascertain as much as you can, how difficult the situation is. You can get a message to my teamster, let me know when you're ready for help and how many men you'll need. You could kind of wander into the general store and slip a note to my driver. Say around eleven in the morning four days from now. That'd be Tuesday."

"You have two men you can absolutely trust?"

"Yep. I'll be one. Cookie will be the other. That way you'll know who you're lookin' for."

"I dunno. It's taking an awful risk."

"If you go after *El Atrevido* alone, there won't be any risk. Because you won't stand a chance, Texas Ranger or not."

"That means I'll have to keep him in check until the cavalry comes to the rescue."

"I'd prefer you didn't put it quite that way, but yes. Everyone knows how often the United States Cavalry messed things up. Custer at the Little Big Horn being a prime example."

"What about your bosses? They might not appreciate you getting involved."

McDougal snorted. "Those damn tenderfoot Easterners? They've only been here twice. As long as the ranch keeps making money, which it is, they leave me alone. I've pretty much got *carte blanche* on how I run the place."

Will rubbed his jaw, lifted his hat and ran a hand through his hair before answering.

"All right. I'll trust you . . . Duke."

"You won't be sorry, Ranger."

"Will."

"Will. I'll see you in Coffee City on Tuesday. Speaking of coffee, do you want another cup before you go?"

"No, I'd best be on my way. Jonas might already be dead. But if he's not, he might be sooner rather than later. It's better I get to town as quickly as I can."

"You might not be able to get to him, at least until we arrive to help."

"True. But if I'm in town *El Atrevido* might be hesitant to kill another Ranger with me there."

"Or he might just finish you both off."

"That's likely. In which case, you and your men will be Special Rangers with the authority to go after *El Atrevido* and his gang. Consider yourselves sworn in as of right now. Just keep that under your hat until the day comes I send for you."

"Of course."

Will handed Duke his empty mug and climbed back into the saddle.

"*Adios*, Duke."

"*Vaya con Dios*."

19

Will felt the animosity and downright hatred as soon as he rode into Coffee City. The silver star in silver circle badge pinned to his vest glittered defiantly in the late afternoon sun. Even the horses felt the tension. Rebel pulled back on his lead rope, while Pete kept his ears pinned flat and fought the bit.

The hairs on the back of Will's neck prickled as he worked his way through town. Most of the people on the street weren't subtle about their feelings toward the Ranger. They pointed at Will and frowned. Merchants came out of their stores to watch him ride past, some shaking their heads in disapproval. Will could feel them staring at his back. He could only hope one didn't pull a gun and put a bullet in that back.

He seemed motionless in the saddle, but his brown eyes were constantly moving, missing nothing. He stopped to allow both horses a short drink from a trough in front of the feed store, then continued on to the Black Coffee Hotel, which appeared to be the only lodging in town. He dismounted, looped the horses' reins around the hitch rail, then started inside. He hesitated, went back and got his Winchester, then continued into the hotel's lobby.

The Black Coffee's lobby was like those of most frontier lodging establishments, with a plain wooden desk backed by a shelf of pigeonholes, a few couches, chairs, tables, and some potted plants to add a splash of color to the otherwise drab décor. The clerk behind the desk, a tall, cadaverously thin man somewhere in his forties, his thinning dark hair pomaded across his scalp, hazel eyes behind a pair of pince-nez spectacles, gave Will a sullen look when he walked up to the desk.

"What d'ya want, Ranger?"

"A room."

"We're full up."

"You certain?"

"Sure am."

"There certainly are a damn lot of keys hanging up for a hotel that supposedly has no rooms available."

"Let me make things crystal clear, Ranger. We're full up for the likes of you."

"You mean a Ranger?"

"I mean any lawman."

"I suppose that means my pardner isn't staying at your fine establishment. He would have arrived yesterday or earlier today. His name's Jonas Peterson. Blond, blue-eyed, kind of young lookin' to be a Ranger, but he sure enough is one. A damn fine one."

"I ain't seen anyone who looks like that,

let alone someone wearing a Ranger's star."

"That's too bad. It's also too bad that you don't want to rent me a room. Let me put this to you in a way you'll be able to understand. As a state peace officer, I have the authority to requisition, or commandeer if you prefer, a room, without paying for it. An entire floor, or even this entire hotel for that matter. Or you can let me have the same room, at your usual rate. Did you get that through your thick skull?"

Will looked at the pigeonholes.

"Seems as if Room 207 is available. I'll wager it'll be satisfactory. I'll take it. As for how long, just as long as it's necessary. Give me the key. Whether I pay for the room or requisition it is up to you. It's your decision."

The clerk scowled at Will, then abruptly turned the register for him to sign.

"Rate's a dollar a night, in advance."

Will signed the register, then threw two five-dollar pieces onto the desk.

"Here's ten days. I might stay longer. Especially if my pard doesn't turn up. I don't suppose *El Atrevido* resides here in this hotel."

The clerk squinted at Will's scrawled signature.

"No one knows where *El Atrevido* lives, but I can tell you one thing—he's welcome in Coffee City. You aren't."

Will grabbed the clerk's shirtfront and dragged

him across the desk. He held the man's face only inches from his. The clerk was now shaking, sweat breaking out on his forehead.

"What's your name, Mister?"

"It's . . . it's Frederick. Frederick Meyer."

"Listen close, Freddy boy, because I'm only going to say this once. Someone in this town, probably a lot of someones, knows who *El Atrevido* is and where he holes up, which is right here in Coffee City or damn close by. So get word to him I want a meeting. Soon. And if anyone thinks of backshooting me in my bed, I'm a real light sleeper, with a nervous trigger finger. Remember that."

Will shoved Meyer backwards, causing him to hit the pigeonholes, then fall to the floor.

"I appreciate your hospitality, Frederick."

Will took the horses to the nearest livery stable, three blocks from the hotel. The owner was a red-headed, blue-eyed young man with the unlikely name of Davis D. Davis. His attitude was decidedly different from the clerk at the hotel. He greeted Will with a cheery "Howdy" and a wide grin across his freckled face.

"Boarding two horses?" he asked.

"Yep. One's my partner's. I hope to catch up with him soon. I have to ask, what's the middle D stand for?"

"Davis," Davis answered, with a chuckle. "My

folks didn't have much imagination when namin' me."

"I would say not," Will answered, also chuckling. "I don't know how long I'll be in town. A week for certain, mebbe longer. My paint's Pete. Jonas's sorrel is Rebel. Treat 'em right."

"All the horses in my care get treated right. Grain twice a day, plenty of hay, and fresh water. Rubdowns every other day. The farrier's right down the alley if their feet need attention. Board's fifty cents per day, per animal."

"That sounds fair."

Will dug in his pocket and pulled out a ten-dollar gold coin.

"Here's ten days. Will that do?"

"It'll do just fine, Ranger."

Will removed his saddlebags, tossed them over his right shoulder, and picked up his rifle.

"Where's a good place to eat around here?"

"Luisa's Place. It's Mexican food, but damn good Mexican food. When you leave here take a left. Luisa's is two blocks down on the right. Tell her I sent you."

"I'll do that. Obliged. One last thing."

"What's that?"

"Can you tell me anything about *El Atrevido*?"

"The Daring One? About as much as anyone else can. He's a good man to steer clear of. And he's got a lot of *amigos* in this town. Don't tell me you're after *him?*"

"I sure as blazes am. I believe he's got my partner. I intend to get him back."

Davis sighed.

"You didn't hear this from me. No one is really certain who *El Atrevido* is. Some say he's Anglo, others Mexican, maybe a half-breed. He's got a bunch of men workin' for him. Rumor has it they stay at an old, abandoned rancho right on the banks of the Rio Grande. Anyone who's tried to find out exactly where at either disappears, or turns up dead. Just to give you an idea what you're up against."

"*Gracias*, Mr. Davis Davis Davis. The only thing we discussed is horses."

Will enjoyed a tasty supper at Luisa's. He decided to forego visiting any of the saloons until the next night. Instead, he went back to his room, cleaned his guns, then went to bed. He lay staring at the ceiling for quite some time.

I sure ain't gonna find much help in this town. El Atrevido*'s seen to that. I can't really blame anyone. Folks either look at him as almost the Second Coming, or they're too afraid to stand up to him. I don't have a clue as to who he is, or where to find him, except somewhere near the river. My first order of business is finding Jonas, if he hasn't already been killed and dumped into the Rio.*

Will sighed.

I hope spreading the word I'm after El Atrevido *will have him come lookin' for me. That'll be a helluva lot easier than me looking for a needle in a damn big haystack. Tomorrow I start poking around.*

He finally drifted into a restless sleep.

The temperature hadn't dropped much after the sun went down, so Will had left his window open to catch the breeze off the river. The sound of the rolling water and the fluttering of the curtains lulled him into a deeper sleep. Sometime after midnight he was awakened by a new, different sound. He strained to determine what it was, then recognized it as the bump of a ladder being placed against the wall underneath his window, soon followed by the footsteps of someone climbing that ladder.

Will eased his Colt Peacemaker from its holster on the bedside table. He waited until just the top of the climber's head appeared in the window, then thumbed back the hammer and pulled the trigger. His bullet scraped across the intruder's scalp. The man yelped in shock and surprise, tumbled off the ladder, and hit the soft ground. By the time Will reached the window, the man was already up and running, his footsteps fading away toward the river.

Will listened for a few moments. Either no one had heard his shot, or those who had stayed safely behind closed doors. He shrugged, pushed the ladder over, and closed the window. After replacing the spent cartridge, he climbed back into bed.

I guess that was my welcome greeting from El Atrevido. *I'd bet my hat it won't be too long until I hear from him again.*

20

As much as he wanted to locate *El Atrevido*'s headquarters, and more importantly find Jonas, Will decided to spend the next day questioning people in Coffee City. After all, even if he learned the location of *El Atrevido*'s rancho, it would be impossible to tackle the outlaw's gang single-handedly. If luck was with him, the outlaw chief would send someone after him again. This time, Will would be ready. He'd take any would-be killer alive and make him talk, one way or another.

With most of the residents of Coffee City of the belief *El Atrevido* was robbing the wealthy, then distributing his ill-gotten gains to the peons, or too afraid of him to talk for fear of facing The Daring One's wrath, Will learned little.

After having supper, again at Luisa's, he went to the *Queso Fresca* Cantina. When he stopped at the bar the patrons on either side moved away, giving him a wide berth. Clearly they were aware he was a target of *El Atrevido*, and they didn't intend to be struck by a bullet meant for the Ranger. The bartender was surly, but did serve Will, quickly placing his drinks on the bar then scurrying to serve other patrons. He was terrified, whether of being accidentally shot when Will was attacked, or because if he was caught serving the Ranger he would face the wrath of *El Atrevido* Will couldn't know.

Will drank two shots of fiery tequila, and was nursing his second beer when a man came up on his left.

"Y'know, this is *El Atrevido*'s town. He treats folks good. We ain't gonna allow any Ranger to take him in."

He started to reach for his gun. Before he could even grasp its handle, Will had pulled out his Peacemaker and rammed the barrel into the man's belly, causing him to grunt.

"You want me to pull this trigger?"

"No. No, please."

"Then you get a message to your boss."

"I don't work for him."

"But I'm willing to bet you know someone who does, or how to reach him. You tell him I'm gonna take him down. I might die tryin', but not until after he's dead, and as many of his men as I can take with me. And if he's holding onto my partner, he'd better turn him loose, and not half dead. If Jonas is already dead, or turns up that way, I'll slice *El Atrevido* into little pieces of fish bait. I'll cut off his *cojones* first, then his fingers, ears, nose, and toes. Then I'll take his scalp. After that I'll carve out his guts. He'll die the longest, slowest, most painful death imaginable. You tell him that."

Will grabbed the man by the shoulder, spun him around, and shoved him through the batwings to land face down in the street.

"*Camarero, otra cerveza. Ahora.*"

21

Two days later, Will spent the day trying to find *El Atrevido*'s rancho. In the maze of canyons, washes, and river breaks it was an arduous task. He believed he had narrowed down the area which needed to be searched. With sunset approaching, and only being a few miles from Coffee City, Will decided to call it a day and return to town, where there would be far less chance of a drygulcher sneaking up on him in the dark.

He leaned over and patted his horse's neck.

"C'mon, Pete, let's head back in. Looks like we'll have to start all over again come morning."

Pete nickered and shook his head. Will eased him into a walk. They were about two miles from town when Pete shied at a man popping up from seemingly nowhere, as if he had materialized from the dirt itself.

Pete's sudden move saved his rider's life. The ambusher's bullet whined past Will's right ear. Before he could fire again, Pete reared high, then brought his right forehoof down on the man's skull, cracking it open. Pete reared once, twice, three times more before Will was able to bring him under control, each time his hooves slamming down on the ambusher's shattered corpse.

"Enough, Pete! He's had enough."

Pete stood, snorting and blowing while Will dismounted and examined the body.

"Even his own mother wouldn't recognize this *hombre*, Pete. Thanks, pard. Extra oats for you tonight."

Pete nuzzled Will's shoulder.

Will looked around for a horse, but there was none to be found.

"Seems as if the *hombre* walked here, wherever he came from. Dollars to doughnuts he was at *El Atrevido*'s rancho. I reckon it's not far off. We'll just leave this bastard here for his *amigos* to pick him up, or the scavengers to take care of him, whoever gets here first. I'd purely love to try'n follow his trail, but it's gettin' dark fast, and there might be some others out in the *malpais* waiting to get us in their sights. We'll pick up the trail come morning. It'd be great to pin down the rancho's location before we meet Duke McDougal day after tomorrow."

Will returned to town, got Pete settled, had his supper, and was crossing the street to reach his hotel when two men blocked his way. One was big, at least six feet four inches tall, well above average height for the times, and weighing around two hundred and forty pounds. His left eye was half closed by an old knife scar. The other was tall and lanky, his straw-colored hair and pale blue eyes in stark contrast to his partner's dark features.

"Hey, Ranger. We've got a message for you from *El Atrevido*," the big man said.

Will tensed, not knowing what was coming.

"Oh yeah. What is it?"

"This."

The big man launched a roundhouse punch that caught Will squarely on the jaw, knocking him down. Will lay in the street for a moment, shaking his head to clear it. He somehow managed to get to his feet, despite his blurred vision and no sense of balance.

"Here's my reply!"

Will drove a low blow to the big man's groin. The outlaw grabbed his crotch and dropped to his knees, howling in pain. The lanky outlaw hit Will with a sucker punch to his back, directly over his left kidney. Paralyzed with pain, Will fell face down. The lanky outlaw kicked him in the ribs, flipping him over. He drove his boot into Will's belly, driving all the air from his lungs and doubling him up. The big man regained his feet, kicked Will in the back, rolling him face down. Will managed to cover his head against a series of kicks and blows from both men.

"Get out of town," he was told. "You've been warned."

They disappeared into the dark. Not one person came to Will's aid. Coffee City had no marshal, relying instead on the Val Verde County Sheriff's Office. They only came into town at a report of trouble. Since the deaths of the sheriff and three of his deputies left the county with only two deputies after the raid on Del Rio, and with Coffee City under the control of *El Atrevido*, no one dared to ask for local authorities to intervene.

Will wasn't certain how long it was until he was able to stand up, pick up his saddlebags from where they had fallen, and stagger to his room. The climb up the stairs to the second floor seemed to take half the night. Once he closed the door behind him, he braced a chair against it, lit the bedside lamp, then got his medical from his saddlebags. He pulled off his boots, stripped off his clothes, washed out the cuts and scrapes he'd suffered, rubbed witch hazel over the bruises which covered most of his upper body and face. At least it appeared he hadn't suffered any broken bones. Once finished, he stumbled to his bed and collapsed face down across the mattress.

22

Will was awakened by someone pounding on his door and shouting his name. He shook his head to clear the cobwebs from his brain. It took him a moment to realize where he was. The room was dark, except for the dim light cast by the turned low coal oil lamp. The sky outside his window was still pitch black, with no sign of dawn approaching.

"Ranger! It's Dale Harvey, the night clerk. Are you in there? I need to see you right now!"

Unlike the day clerk, Meyer, Harvey had treated Will courteously, as he would any paying guest.

"Gimme a minute," Will answered. He sat on the edge of the bed, picked up his denims from where he'd dropped them on the floor and pulled them on. As a precaution, he took his Colt from its holster. He padded barefoot to the door.

"You alone, Dale?"

"Yeah. Hurry your damn butt out here."

Will opened the door. Harvey appeared flustered.

"Come with me."

"Let me finish getting dressed."

"You don't have that much time. Let's move."

Harvey hurried Will down the stairs so quickly

that, several times, he nearly lost his balance and fell.

"Over here," Harvey said, once they reached the lobby.

He led Will to one of the couches. Will stopped short. The man lying there was his missing partner. His almost unrecognizable missing partner.

"Jonas! Is he dead?"

Both of Jonas's eyes were blackened and swollen shut. There was a cut so deep over his left cheek the bone was exposed. His lips were twice their normal size, coated with dried blood. His nose was broken, twisted to one side. Jonas's jaw had a large, purplish black bruise running the entire length of its right side. There was still a lump at the base of his skull where he'd been clubbed. His breathing was ragged, his skin pale and cool to the touch.

"Not yet, but I dunno why he isn't," Harvey answered. "Someone really worked him over. I've already sent the *hombre* who brought him in for the doctor. They should be back any minute."

Harvey finally noticed Will's battered face and bruised body.

"I'd wager the same men who beat your partner nigh unto death are the same ones who got to you. You don't look all that healthy either."

"I'll manage."

Will placed a hand on Jonas's shoulder. A man,

particularly a lawman, was not supposed to show his emotions. Crying in public was especially frowned upon. Will couldn't help himself as he looked at his badly beaten partner and friend. He choked up. Tears rolled down his cheeks.

"Jonas. Can you hear me?"

No response.

"Jonas, it's Will. Can you hear me? Who did this to you?"

A slight moan.

"Jonas, I promise you I'll find the damn bastards and make them pay. There's nowhere on God's green Earth they can hide. When I catch up to them, I'll do to them exactly what they did to you, only I'll make certain to finish the job. You hang in there, pal. You'll pull through. You're too stubborn a son of a bitch to die."

Will broke off when two men rushed into the lobby, one an elderly Mexican, the other a young man carrying a black doctor's bag.

"I'm Doctor Phineas Holloway. Please step aside so I might examine the patient."

"Do everything you can for him, Doc," Will pleaded. "He's got to be all right."

Holloway glanced at the badge pinned to Will's vest, the one pinned to Jonas's torn and bloodstained shirt.

"I'll do all that's humanly possible, Ranger," he assured Will. "However, just by looking at him, I can say he's very badly injured."

"That's all I ask, Doc."

"Mr. Harvey, if you could get water boiling and plenty of clean towels. I'm going to need them. Along with some pans. Also a bottle of whiskey."

"I'll get started on those right now, Doctor."

Holloway skinned open Jonas's eyelids to examine his pupils.

"One good sign. His pupils aren't fixed and dilated."

He took Jonas's pulse and checked his temperature.

"His pulse is good, strong and steady. I am concerned about his breathing. I'm also quite worried about possible internal injuries or hemorrhaging. I'm going to check for any signs of those, or any broken bones, before I begin treating his obvious injuries. Ranger, if you could help me lift him to a sitting position for just a moment, I need to remove his shirt and vest."

"Of course."

Will slid his hands under Jonas's shoulders to sit him up. Doctor Holloway removed the vest and shirt, then nodded at Will, who gently laid Jonas back down. Holloway handed Will Jonas's shirt and vest.

Will went to place the garments on a nearby ladder-backed chair. He noticed a piece of paper stuffed into the vest's left breast pocket. He pulled it out and unfolded it.

By now you should have received my second

warning. Consider yourself fortunate I ordered my men not to kill you. This is your first. By the time you read this note, your fellow Ranger will be dead. I will give you one day to bury him, then leave Coffee City. I and my entire organization will arrive in Coffee City at seven in the morning the day after tomorrow. If you are not gone, we will kill you and destroy the town, burning it to the ground. I have already sent a message to the citizens, warning them of what will happen if you refuse to depart. No one defies El Atrevido*!*

Will cursed, started to crumple the paper, then thought better of it. The note could be invaluable evidence if *El Atrevido* was captured and stood trial. Not that Will intended for him to live that long. Not after what he'd had done to Jonas. He'd make certain of that. *El Atrevido* was a walking dead man.

He folded the paper and slid it into his vest pocket.

Will started when Jonas gave a soft cry.

"What happened, Doc?"

"I just pushed his nose back into place so he can breathe more easily. He's still unconscious. It's better he remain in a coma for the next twenty-four hours."

"I'm going to speak with the man who brought him in. We'll be right outside. Send the clerk for me if anything changes."

"Will do."

Will nodded to the elderly Mexican.

"*Hablas Ingles*?"

"*Si, Senor*."

"Come outside and have a quirly."

"*Gracias*."

Will and the old man went onto the hotel's front porch. Will rolled two quirlies, lit them, and handed one to the Mexican.

"My name's Will Kirkpatrick. What is yours?"

"Juan Valdez."

"Jonas is my partner. Where did you find him?"

"I did not exactly find him. I live alone, across the border, about eleven kilometers from here. I am an old man, who only wishes to work my small farm in peace. I have nothing, so *El Atrevido* lets me be, except for when his men take eggs without paying me. However, some of his men came to my home earlier. They forced me to bring my mule and wagon to the Texas side of the *Rio Bravo*. There they put your *amigo* in my wagon. I was ordered to bring him here. They believed he was dead, or soon would be. I felt he was a fighter, and would not die so easily as they believed. I got here as fast as Tecate could move."

"You know you can never go back home. They will not want you alive as a possible witness."

"*Si*, I know that. Which is why I brought my dog with me. My only other animals are a few chickens and goats, which live off the land.

I hope to be far from here before the time The Daring One gave you is up."

"You won't be. Not traveling by mule-drawn wagon."

"I know, but I must try."

"Would you be willing to stay and fight?"

"You would ask that of an old man?"

"Age doesn't matter. Spirit does. You just might have saved my pard's life. That shows you have spirit. What do you say? I'll need every man and woman I can get when The Daring One raids Coffee City. Very few, if any, will help me. Jonas won't be able to fight. He may yet die. I have help coming from outside, but we will still be greatly outnumbered. Unless you know where *El Atrevido* has his hideout. I'd prefer to fight him there, and not involve so many innocent folks."

"I don't know exactly, but I do know it would be impossible to fight him there. It's in one of the deep canyons, well-guarded. The terrain makes it impossible to approach undetected, let alone mount an attack. He has access to the *rio*, so has water to withstand a siege and an easy path to safety in Mexico if necessary. If you are going to make a stand, I am afraid you will have to make it here. And I will stand with you."

"*Gracias*, *Senor Valdez*. Listen, I'll be staying with Jonas for the night. Then, I'll have to deal with the people of this town. Me'n Jonas have

Room 207. Here's the key. Go get yourself some rest. I'm obliged for you bringing Jonas here. I'm sorry it puts you in the middle. Take your rig to Mr. Davis at the stable down the way. Tell him you are with us. We will pay for boarding your mule."

"*Dios* has a plan for everyone. He placed me here for a reason. I have faith in Him, and will accept whatever fate He has waiting for me. I will pray that His will be done."

"Add me and Jonas to your prayers, *por favor*."

"As you wish."

"*Muchas Gracias*."

Valdez shuffled to his wagon. Will went back inside.

Doctor Holloway and Dale Harvey were still ministering to Jonas. The physician was taking the final stitches to the cut on Jonas's cheek.

"How's he doin', Doc?" Will asked.

"He's holding his own, which is all that can be expected. I've done all I can do for now. If you'll kindly sit down, I'll treat your injuries."

"I'm not hurt that bad, Doc."

"Let me be the judge of that. Especially since it's obvious you'll soon have a fight on your hands."

Will sighed.

"A bigger one than you can imagine. All right, I guess I do need some patchin' up."

Will settled into the nearest chair. More

exhausted than he realized, he immediately fell asleep, and awoke only briefly while Holloway worked on him. Once the doctor was finished, Will stretched out on the floor, alongside the couch where Jonas was fighting for his life.

23

The sun rose blood red the day *El Atrevido* had promised to kill Will and wipe out the town of Coffee City. At this early hour, when merchants would normally be preparing to open and people beginning their day, the town was unusually quiet, the streets empty. Quite a number of people had left town, some planning to remain just beyond the city limits until they saw what developed, others making the trip to Del Rio.

As he'd promised, Duke McDougal arrived with eight men, including himself and Cookie. Will had managed to convince a few residents of Coffee City to help defend their home. Dale Harvey, the night clerk at the hotel, was one. So was Davis D. Davis, the livery stable owner. Solomon Lebowitz, who owned the Coffee City Mercantile, and his teenaged son Nehemiah were hunkered down in the store, rifles in hand and plenty of spare ammunition.

Sam Langdon, the card sharp who ran the biggest gambling parlor in town, offered to defend his establishment. John "Jolly" Rogers, a former Navy seaman and now the town's blacksmith and farrier, was also in place at his shop. Will's most unusual recruit was Sophia Hudspeth, the town dressmaker and milliner. She had spent most of the previous day and night creating realistic looking gunfighter mannequins out of dressmakers' forms, then strategically placing them in windows where they would be seen easily behind the thin curtains which blurred their features. Those decoys not only made it appear Coffee City had more defenders than *El Atrevido* and his men expected, but would also be tempting targets, drawing the attention of gunmen away from the actual defenders, causing them to waste valuable ammunition in the process.

Once she'd completed her task, Sophia declared she was not about to be left out of the upcoming fight. She settled into a niche between her shop and the dry goods store, armed with a well-worn Greener shotgun.

At quarter to seven, Will made one last round of the town. He finished with checking on Jonas, who, still too weak to fight, had been moved upstairs to the hotel room he and Will shared. Juan Valdez would remain with him, prepared to fight off anyone who might breach the room.

Doctor Holloway was standing by in his home office, ready to tend to the wounded, pronounce those killed officially dead once everything was settled, no matter which side prevailed.

Will walked to where the main road came in from the northwest. His Peacemaker, the usually empty chamber under the hammer now loaded, was loose in its holster. He held his Winchester on his right shoulder. He stood in the middle of the street, waiting as the minutes ticked away.

At precisely two minutes before seven, he heard the hoofbeats of fast approaching horses. A group of at least twenty-five masked or hooded riders swept into view, led by one mounted on a shiny black gelding. Will aimed his rifle at that one. Sliding the black to a rearing stop, the leader ordered the riders to halt.

"I see you didn't take my warning, Ranger," the leader growled, voice muffled through the hood. "I guess you've decided it's a good day to die."

"It's not," Will answered. "No day's a good day to die. No Indian ever said that, neither. Another falsehood spread by whites like me. No person, man or woman, ever thinks it's a good day to die. Any dyin' here today won't be done by me. It's high time your terrorizing the good people of this section of Texas and Mexico comes to a stop. I'm the man who's gonna do just that."

He levered and fired his rifle. The leader's horse shied just as he pulled the trigger. Will's bullet hit a man behind instead. Shot through the chest, the first of *El Atrevido*'s men thudded dead to the street. The rest scattered.

Will dove to his belly and rolled under the cover of a buckboard as gunfire erupted. Bullets raked the street, men shouting, horses neighing in fear and confusion. A scream from behind him told Will one of his men had taken a bullet, how badly he was hit Will had no way of knowing. He was too busy trying not to take a bullet himself. He shot another man out of the saddle, then slid under the boardwalk. Under its shelter, he belly-crawled backward, slid back out in front of the hotel, came up firing. He got one man in the belly, another in the back, then a bullet struck him in the side. He staggered into the hotel's lobby.

Gunfire continued unabated. Two blasts from a shotgun, the shattering of glass, followed by screams of pain, indicated Sophia Hudspeth had made good on her promise to fight with the others.

More windows shattered as gunmen fired at the decoy targets Sophia had made. Leaving themselves exposed while they blazed away at the decoys made them easy targets for Duke McDougal and the men of the Circle H. They brought down at least eight men. The Circle H did lose one man, Joel Williams, who took a bullet in the brain.

The gunfire was becoming more sporadic now. A splinter group of *El Atrevido*'s men, numbering eight including The Daring One, forced their way into the hotel's lobby, where Will and Harvey were the only defenders. Outnumbered four to one, Will and the desk clerk fought furiously, gunning down half the group before Harvey caught a bullet in his chest. Will killed the man who'd gotten Harvey with a bullet through the throat, then a red-hot poker seemed to rip through his guts. He clawed at his bullet-torn belly, managed to get off one more shot, which plowed harmlessly into the floor. He folded in half, slammed face down to the floor, and passed out.

"I told you today would be the day you die, Ranger!" *El Atrevido* shouted in triumph.

Bullets rained down from the fourth-floor balcony, cutting down the rest of *El Atrevido*'s gang, as Jonas, barely able to stand, leaning against the railing for support, and Valdez got into the fight.

Silence descended on Coffee City, broken only by the sound of hard ridden horses leaving town as the few survivors of *El Atrevido*'s gang fled. Valdez and Jonas worked their way down the stairs. Jonas hobbled straight over to where Will lay, used the last of his strength to roll Will onto his back.

"He's still alive, but hurt real bad," Jonas said to Valdez.

Valdez straightened up from checking Dale Harvey.

"This man is beyond help. I will go find the *medico* for your partner."

"*Gracias*."

Several of the defenders, including Sophia Hudspeth, wandered into the hotel. Jonas ordered three to check on the men lying in the street, seeing if any were still alive and in need of medical treatment. He and the others began searching the dead in the hotel lobby.

When Jonas came to *El Atrevido*, he pulled off the gang leader's mask. The Daring One glared at him with hate-filled eyes. Jonas jumped back in surprise, both at the fact the outlaw was still alive, and at whom he was looking.

"Jennifer! *You* are The Daring One?"

"Yes. Why are you surprised? I'm not the only female outlaw Texas has ever seen."

Jennifer lifted her short-barreled Colt and aimed it at Jonas's chest. Jonas aimed his own gun at her, but couldn't bring himself to pull the trigger, unable to kill a woman, even if it meant his own death.

Two shots rang out, both striking Jennifer in the face, turning its pretty features into a mushy pulp. Jonas turned to see Sophia Hudspeth holding a smoking Derringer.

"Thanks, ma'am," he said. "I . . . I just couldn't kill her."

"Even though she was about to blow you to Kingdom Come. That's just so typical of you damn men, always thinking with your balls rather than your brains. I should have just let her do it."

Jonas was speechless, unable to laugh at or be shocked by the sixtyish widow's language. He settled for falling back into a chair as Doctor Holloway came through the door.

24

Will awoke in his hotel room four days later. Jonas and Doctor Holloway were with him.

"It's high time you woke up, lazy bones," Jonas said.

"It's lucky you woke up at all, Ranger Kirkpatrick," Holloway said. "A bullet in the side and another clean through most of your intestines. Five years ago that would have killed any man. Even using Doctor Goodfellow's method of treating belly wounds, as I did, most men would not have survived being as badly shot. You beat the odds."

"But what happened? Is *El Atrevido* still on the loose?"

"You may tell him, Ranger Peterson, but keep it short," Holloway said.

"No. She's dead. Along with most of her gang."

"She?"

"Yep. Jennifer Coltraine."

"Jennifer from the hotel in Del Rio?"

"The same. Once you're feeling a bit better I'll tell you the whole sorry story, including how she trapped and nearly killed me."

"I hate to say this, pard, but you're easy prey for any pretty woman to trap."

"I hate to admit it, but you're right."

"Rest of the story."

"She used the desk clerk job as cover, and to get leads on people worth ambushing and robbing. Most times she led the raids herself, others she gave orders to her men. Anyone who didn't follow them wound up with a bullet in the back."

"Who killed her?"

"It wasn't me. I couldn't do it, even though she had me dead to rights. Sophia Hudspeth put two bullets in her head."

"How many people did we lose?"

"Wrap it up, Ranger," Holloway said.

"Seven all told, plus five wounded. You were hurt the worst. But *El Atrevido*'s reign of terror is finished. A few of her men took off for parts unknown. We didn't have anyone to follow them. They're most likely in either New Mexico Territory or Mexico itself by now. Juan Valdez said to let you know he's grateful to be able to return home."

"As grateful as I am for his help, I hope."

Will yawned and stretched, letting out a yip of pain.

"That's all, both of you," Holloway ordered. "If you break open my stitches, Ranger Kirkpatrick, you most likely will die, despite all my efforts. I'll check on you again this evening. Now go back to sleep. I mean both of you."

"The best advice I've heard in a long time,"

Will said. "Jonas, seems as if you get to do the paperwork this time."

"Sure. You take the easy way to wriggle out of it by getting yourself shot in the guts. Some pardner you are."

"One more word from either of you and I'll give you both enough laudanum to keep you unconscious for a week," Holloway warned. "I'm not leaving this room until you're both sleeping."

"He's the doctor, Will."

"I reckon he is."

Will let his eyes close. The job was done. He and Jonas had survived. Once they were recovered enough to ride again, they would hit the trail back to Sweetwater, and their next adventure.

Author's Note

The Coffee City in this story is fictional. There is an actual Coffee City in Henderson County, Texas, which was established in the 1960s. It has no connection to the persons or events in this novel.

Center Point Large Print
600 Brooks Road / PO Box 1
Thorndike, ME 04986-0001 USA

(207) 568-3717

US & Canada:
1 800 929-9108
www.centerpointlargeprint.com